P9-AGC-508

THE GARB OF TRUTH

By Ian Stuart

THE GARB OF TRUTH

IAN STUART

PUBLISHED FOR THE CRIME CLUB BY
DOUBLEDAY & COMPANY, INC.
GARDEN CITY, NEW YORK
1984

All the characters in this book
are fictitious, and any resemblance
to actual persons, living or dead,
is purely coincidental.

Library of Congress Cataloging in Publication Data
Stuart, Ian.
    The garb of truth.
    I. Title.
PR6069.T77G3   1984   823'.914
ISBN 0-385-19357-2

Library of Congress Catalog Card Number 83-20537
Copyright © 1982 by Ian Stuart
All rights reserved
Printed in the United States of America
First edition in the United States of America

To Celia Dale

"Malice often takes the garb of truth."
—William Hazlitt.

THE GARB OF TRUTH

ONE

It was hot. So hot the heat shimmered along the bonnet of my open TR7, and the metal of the door burned my arm through my sleeve when I rested it there. I swore under my breath and moved my arm away.

The dashboard clock said ten forty-three and, according to the forecasters, by lunch-time the temperature would be twenty-five—nearly eighty degrees Fahrenheit. And this was only the second week of May.

The morning rush-hour was long past, but at the round-about where the dual carriageway came down from the M1, cars were queuing a hundred yards back. I slowed to a halt behind an elderly Cortina and waited.

In the flats across the road, somebody was playing the bag-pipes. It was music for the hills and glens, out of place amidst the brick and concrete of a new town, but the lament, infinitely sad, fitted my mood. I told myself it was absurd to feel humiliated; I had been promoted. But people—Laura, my colleagues, people in the bank I hardly knew—expected me to get Bill Sale's job when he left Cornish Street. The grape-vine said I would. Now I wasn't getting it. Instead I was being given a temporary upgrading, somebody else would go to Cornish Street and in a month or two I would be back where I was yesterday. People would say there must be a question-mark against me.

They would wonder what it was. All except Laura. I wasn't looking forward to telling her. She had wanted me to get the job so badly. Not for herself or the extra money, but because she loved me and wanted things to go well for me. Especially I didn't want her to be troubled just now, when she already had so much to worry her: Yesterday her mother had gone into hospital for tests. The doctors feared she had cancer, and Laura was staying with her father for a few days to help him and be near the hospital.

Until this morning I had told myself I didn't really care if I got the job or not. Now I knew I had been deceiving myself. I had wanted it badly. It was nearly three years since I joined the Inspection team, and although that was twelve months less than the usual stint, it was long enough for me to wonder what was coming next and to take a personal interest in any sub-manager's post that came up.

The Chief himself had let me know I was in line for something before long, and when the letter came instructing me to report to district office to see Brian Anniss, the district staff manager, it had seemed to clinch it.

So much for my expectations. Cornish Street wasn't even mentioned.

I should have known when I saw the Chief with him; Hudson wouldn't have been there if I was on the point of leaving his department. But I didn't, and I listened with a growing feeling of disillusionment while Anniss explained that it had been decided to reorganize the work of Inspection in the district and left it to the Chief to explain.

John Parker would continue to be the district inspector, but in future there would be four small teams working more or less autonomously under his overall control. Charles Harrison would be the full inspector leading one of them, but he was still on sick-leave recovering from a mild heart attack. Until he was fit to return I would deputize for him. For so long I would be an acting inspector. Unpaid.

"With luck, Charles will be back in a month or so," the

Chief said. I wasn't sure whether or not that was a reflection on me. "But it'll be good experience for you, David." George Hudson paused and regarded me steadily from under his shaggy brows, his head slightly lowered and thrust forward. It made him look a little like a Highland bull but a good deal fiercer. "I'll tell you, I thought about it for a long time before I recommended you for the job. You know why, don't you?"

I knew all right. He meant I went off the rails sometimes. Not with women or drinking too much, but following my own ideas and getting involved in matters which weren't strictly part of the job. Because of that, they hadn't been able to quietly bury the Alec Sanders business. Perhaps it would have been better if I'd left it alone; none of us had enjoyed the judge's comments at the trial. They had been unjustified and spoken in ignorance, but the press had seized on them with relish; any criticism of a bank with the authority of one of Her Majesty's judges behind it was meat and drink to them.

The Chief gave me a final stare, which seemed thoughtful, rather than overtly hostile, and grunted. I understood; for as long as it took Charles to recover, I was on probation.

They had expected me to be pleased. Perhaps I should be. After all, there weren't many full inspectors, even acting unpaid ones, as young as thirty-three, and if I kept my nose clean the experience must count in my favour when the next job came up. They didn't know I wanted to get back to a branch, to belong somewhere and have my own canoe to paddle instead of spending my days in a nomadic existence, checking other people's work, unwelcomed and, too often, mildly resented.

The balding driver of the Cortina lit a cigarette and threw the empty packet out of the window. I watched it land in the road and lie there, a tiny addition to the nation's litter. I felt like getting out and throwing it back at him; perhaps because

I was fed up, his casual indifference offended me. But it was
too hot and, anyway, I lacked the moral courage.

We were almost up to the roundabout now. The Cortina
moved forward a few feet, slowed again, then accelerated over
to the comparative shelter of the central island, across the
path of a small Bedford van. The van's driver hooted angrily.

I took advantage of another break in the stream of traffic
and drove on, turning left down the hill, past the neat verges,
the two-storeyed brick houses and flats of a vast housing estate. There was another roundabout at the bottom of the hill,
where six roads met and traffic tied itself in knots round a
series of satellite islands painted on the tarmac. Two sky-
scraper office blocks marked the boundary of the town centre.
I turned right, avoided an MGB that seemed intent on ram-
ming me and swung left at the next corner.

Lemsfield had blended the old and new more successfully
than most of the post-war new towns. Perhaps the river,
hardly more than a brook flowing gently across a wide, flat
expanse of grass, served as a unifying influence, drawing old
and new together. Beyond the quarter-mile of vulgar shop
fronts, past the civic hall with its plate glass and fluted roof
and up a low hill, you came to streets where narrow buildings
jostled each other along the pavements and the pubs had
hardly changed in two centuries.

The bank was in a crescent of shops and other banks between the river and the main street, which, for some obscure
and probably pretentious reason, was known as the Ridings.
The High Street was half a mile away in the Old Town. I
parked in the car-park on the other side of the river and
walked back, passing a news agent's with a placard outside
proclaiming, "NATO CRISIS LATEST." I had heard about
the crisis on the radio news, driving over. It had begun with
the defection of a senior official in the West German defence
ministry and the subsequent discovery that he had been a

KGB officer for twenty years. Similar defections had happened before, but this time the official had had access to vital American military secrets and details of their intelligence network throughout Europe. Now the Americans were threatening to withhold information from the other NATO countries and to reduce their commitment to Western European defence. As much as I thought about it at all, I supposed it would all be sorted out eventually; such difficulties always were.

Lemsfield was a large branch with a staff of nearly forty. Externally the building was undistinguished: a flat red brick and glass façade with as little character as a supermarket. The interior was more impressive, the banking-hall rose the height of two storeys with a mezzanine floor overlooking it. But the feeling of light and space was an illusion; when the branch was built, in the mid-fifties, nobody had forseen how rapidly its business would grow, and behind the counter everything had a cramped, make-shift look.

I showed my letter of identification to the girl at the enquiries desk and she pressed the button to release the catch on the security door. I walked through and met Millie Gant, the manager's secretary, coming out of his room. We knew each other slightly, having played mixed doubles together in the area tennis team two or three times. She went to let him know I had arrived.

He kept me waiting five minutes. There was nobody with him and he wasn't on the phone. It was his way of letting me know he was the manager and emphasizing the difference in our standing. I was young enough—or, perhaps, conceited enough—to resent it. Then Millie came to tell me I could go in. She smiled as she said it.

The manager's room was the only part of the branch behind the counter to give an impression of spaciousness, but Robert Waites dominated it. He was a big man with a high, domed brow and strangely pale blue eyes set in fleshy cheeks stained too ripely by high blood-pressure. I had heard that his appearance and his slow, weighty way of speaking impressed people who didn't know him well.

It was the first time we had met. He didn't offer to shake hands, and for several seconds we eyed each other warily across his desk. He didn't ask me to sit down either; he was already sitting. Apart from an almost empty wire basket, there was nothing on the desk to indicate work.

"Good day, Mr. Grierson." His voice was plummy. "You come from the North, I believe." It might have been Outer Mongolia, the way he said it.

"County Durham," I told him.

"Yes." He had made a gesture; now he dismissed any pretence of interest. "Well, no doubt we shall see a good deal of each other while you're here. I hope you people will cause as little disruption as you can; this is a busy branch and we are understaffed."

I happened to know that in fact it was two over its nominal strength and wished that, just for once, a manager would tell me he had more staff than he needed.

"We always do that," I told him, not caring much if my annoyance showed. I had never before been asked in so many words not to be a nuisance. Most managers accepted that we had a job to do and left us to get on with it. Anyway, an inspector who deliberately caused friction would be asking for trouble.

Waites regarded me from under his heavy eyelids for several seconds. "I'm sure you will," he agreed at last. He made it sound like a warning. "Well, I mustn't keep you; I'm sure you have a lot to be getting on with."

I had been dismissed, and with a murmur he was free to interpret how he liked, I left him. The rest of the team had finished checking the cash in the tills and the reserve safe and were settling down to the tasks which would occupy them for most of the two weeks or so the inspection would last: checking the impersonal accounts and the controls, assessing the advances, checking securities and interviewing the staff. They might refer to us without malice as "the narks," but there was one sense in which our work did resemble that of the police: it was 99 per cent perspiration and only 1 per cent inspiration.

Ken Leach told me Ben and Trevor were in the strong-room checking the share certificates and other securities against the entries in the registers. It was tedious, unrewarding work, but it had to be done. The strong-room at Lemsfield was down a steep flight of concrete steps, and the massive outer door was standing open, but the grille between the first room, where only old books and ledgers were stored, and the strong-room proper was locked. Ben saw me and came across to let me in.

"How did it go?" he asked. He was the more uninhibited of the two; Trevor would have waited for me to volunteer information, but even he couldn't bring himself to ask me straight out if I was getting Bill Sale's job.

"It wasn't about Cornish Street," I told him. I didn't want to talk about it yet. Later, when the first disappointment had faded, I would tell them.

Ben gave me a curious look, but he let the subject drop.

"No problems?" I enquired.

"Not so far. One of the tills was a hundred wrong last night, but we found it."

"Have you met God yet?" Trevor asked.

I nodded. "Did you know him before?"

"I was on securities at Langton Pagnell when he was there, worse luck. Stupid old sod."

From his tone I gathered Trevor's time with Waites hadn't been particularly happy; there was an undercurrent of resentment rare in him. Ben laughed.

"I'm going to start the accounts," I told them. "If it's all right with Harry Roche, I'll be in the staff-room."

Roche was the sub-manager. He raised no objections to my using the room; it was large enough for me not to be in the way of the staff at coffee- and lunch-times and far enough away for me to be out of his hair. Sub-managers tended to bear the brunt of any inspection: they were asked and expected to answer most of the questions which arose and, as they were directly responsible for the efficient running of the branch, they felt they were the targets for any criticism there was going. A bad report might delay promotion, possibly blight a whole future. It made some of them very defensive.

I went up to the machine-room, on the first floor. Three girls were seated at computer terminals, while others were filing cheques, dealing with standing orders and sending out statements. I asked the supervisor for what I needed and took myself off to the staff-room next door.

Like most staff-rooms I had seen, this one was about as homely as a railway waiting-room. It was large enough to hold twenty people, but hardly in comfort. Apart from a Baby Belling cooker and an ancient refrigerator, the only furniture consisted of a plastic-topped table, eight metal-and-plastic chairs and, ranged round two of the walls, some low settees in the early stages of dilapidation. Their worn and stained orange upholstery clashed with the bright green plastic of the chairs. An electric fan over the draining-board hummed noisily but did little to dispel the pervasive odours of instant coffee, cigarette smoke and old food. Nobody spent more than ten minutes there for coffee during the morning and half an hour at lunch-time, and it bore all the signs of a room through which people passed briefly, leaving nothing but litter and indifference.

Most of the staff had had their coffee and departed, and there was only one person still there, a slim woman of about thirty-two in a neat pale green dress. Her neatness was the thing you noticed first about her. She had shortish brown hair that shone, a firm jaw and fine grey eyes and, although she wasn't conventionally pretty, she was attractive in a cool, reserved way. Caroline Bedford, the assistant manager, I supposed.

She looked up when I walked in, and there was something mildly disconcerting about the look she gave me. It was neither friendly nor hostile, just wholly uninterested. I said, "Hallo," and sat down at the table. She murmured, "Good morning," and almost immediately stood up, washed her cup at the sink and went out.

I got on with my work.

After a while Harry Roche came to discuss a query Ken Leach had raised. We talked about it for five minutes and he went away satisfied. At twelve-thirty I went to find the others and we took ourselves off to a pub Ben knew for a snack.

TWO

The Lamb Hotel hung its sign over the narrow pavement where it had done for three hundred years. I drove under the arch where once horse-shoes and iron-tyred wheels had rattled across the cobbles and parked near the wall. Through an open window came the clink of crockery and the sounds of women talking in some foreign language.

I had rung Laura at lunch-time. She had arrived safely and gone to the hospital with her mother and father. When I told her about my interview I could hear the disappointment in her voice when she said, "Oh, David, I am sorry." I wished she were here so that I could explain it didn't matter, that there would be other jobs, and what I had been given would be useful experience. Perhaps I would have convinced myself.

The rest of the team lived near enough to go home each day. I could have done the same, but I didn't fancy a forty-minute drive after work merely to enjoy my own company and get my own meal, so I had phoned the Lamb this morning and booked a room for the next four nights. What happened after that depended on whether Laura had returned.

Inside the inn, the sun shone through small leaded panes on dark wood. There was a faint odour of furniture polish.

"I've booked a room," I told the receptionist, a chubby, fair girl of about twenty. "My name's Grierson."

"Oh yes, Mr. Grierson. Number Four. It's on the left up the stairs."

I filled up the card she gave me and climbed the wide

staircase. Number Four was a pleasant, airy room looking across the street to a church half hidden by limes and syca- mores. It had a colour television set, looking slightly out of place beside the heavy, old-fashioned furniture, and a shower, and by the time I had bathed and changed I felt more cheer- ful. I decided I had comfortable time for a drink before din- ner, and afterwards I would have a walk round part of the town. Lemsfield was new ground for me.

It was big enough to have its own daily paper, the Lems- field *Evening Star*. I bought a copy at the reception desk, took it through to the bar and asked the barman for a half of bitter. The lead story was about the NATO crisis. I glanced through it rather perfunctorily, then saw something I had forgotten: that the Minister of Defence was Lemsfield's MP, Gerald Sapsed. Apparently he was due to speak at a public meeting in the civic hall that evening. Not particularly interested, I turned to the back pages and the cricket scores.

I heard the crowd before I saw it. At first it was no more than a distant murmur, a background accompaniment to the sounds of passing traffic, muffled by the intervening buildings. Then I rounded a corner not far from the library, found my- self in the Ridings and saw them. They were on the lower ground in front of the civic hall, a milling, jostling crowd a hundred or more strong. I started walking that way, partly from curiosity and partly because it was the shortest route back to the Lamb.

Most of the crowd were young—student age. They were pushing and shouting, and some of them were waving plac- ards protesting about nuclear arms, NATO and unemploy- ment. A score of policemen were struggling to hold them back from the doors, while others were keeping the pavement more or less clear.

For the most part, the crowd looked good humoured, although there were a few who had the fanatics' glazed stares. I saw a girl of about twenty-five screaming abuse at the police; she looked beside herself with the passion of her convictions. Others were laughing and shouting cheerfully.

I passed a television company's outside broadcast van parked by the kerb, its crew hard at work; dodged their cables draped across the pavement, and walked on.

Gradually the noise faded into the distance, and by the time I reached the outskirts of the Old Town and turned up the side-street towards the hotel, I could no longer hear it. I decided I might as well have a drink, then watch the "News at Ten" on ITV in my room.

The hotel bar at the Lamb appeared to be the meeting-place for those of the more affluent local people who didn't care for the modern pubs in the New Town or the seedier ones in the Old. It had the clubbish atmosphere common to such places, and entering it I felt I was almost an outsider, tolerated but hardly welcome.

At that time on a Monday evening it was half empty. I asked the barman for a pint of bitter and looked round. Most of the customers were middle-aged or elderly, but there was a sprinkling of under-thirties.

"There's something going on outside the civic hall," I remarked to the barman as he pushed my glass across the counter and wiped up the little pool of beer that had overflowed.

He was about forty, small and dark, and he spoke with the suggestion of an Irish accent. "So somebody was saying, sir. It'll be the students. Fifty-four pence, please, sir."

"From the Poly?" I asked, finding the right money amongst the coins in my pocket and handing it to him.

He nodded, seemingly unconcerned—barely even interested. Either they were accustomed to such excitements in Lemsfield or the students inhabited a different world and he had little more contact with them than he would have done if they were on the other side of the universe.

"The MP's speaking there, isn't he?" I said.

"So I believe." He walked away to serve somebody farther along the bar.

I sat on a stool, sipped my beer and watched the other customers—in particular a girl of twenty-two or three with long dark hair, an intriguing smile and a wonderful figure. She made me wish again that Laura were there instead of a hundred miles away.

After five minutes a dark, strongly built man came in, leaned on the bar beside me and called, "A double Bell's, Danny, when you're free."

The barman handed his change to the customer he was serving and came over. "Evening, Mr. Hillyer," he said in the tone, neither quite respectful nor overfamiliar, barmen use when they are talking to people they know well and about whom they have heard a good deal, not all of it creditable. Turning, he held a glass up to the measure. "You haven't gone to the civic hall, then?"

"What do you mean?" For some reason, the question seemed to anger the newcomer.

"I thought maybe you had. There's a lot gone to hear the MP, they say."

Hillyer took out a cheque-book. From the colour, it was one of ours. "Cash me a cheque for twenty quid and take it out of that, will you, Danny?" he said. He had a public school accent.

"I'm sorry, Mr. Hillyer, you know the rules."

"Blast you, Danny. Don't you trust me?"

"It's not that, sir. Mr. Deards won't let us take any cheques without a card. You haven't a card, have you?"

"You know bloody well I haven't."

"It only makes it embarrassing for everybody." Danny didn't look or sound embarrassed, merely firm and quite calm.

"I'll talk to Geoff Deards," Hillyer told him.

"Very good, sir. Shall I fetch him?" Danny started to move away.

"No, another time will do." Hillyer put his cheque-book away, took a pound note from his back pocket and threw it on to the bar.

Danny picked it up impassively and tucked it away in the till. Looking at him, you might have sensed he had scored a small victory but didn't want to make too much of it. Hillyer helped himself to ice, drank nearly half his whisky and looked round.

I was the nearest person to him, and a stranger. It wasn't a position I cared for much; he was the sort of person I usually did my best to avoid, and I looked away to discourage him.

But he wanted company. "Embarrassing, that, eh?" he remarked, seeming no more humiliated than Danny. "Have I seen you before?"

"No," I told him. "I only got here today."

"You're on business?"

I nodded. He wasn't drunk, but it was clear he had had two or three drinks already this evening. Enough to be expansive. Short of being pointedly rude there was nothing I could do but listen.

Eventually, when he wanted to buy me another drink, I declined, said goodnight and went up to my room. The window was wide open and it was much cooler there than in the bar. I switched on the television set, tuned it to the ITV channel and sat down to watch the news.

The headlines promised nothing of absorbing interest, and I picked up the morning's *Telegraph*, scanning the pages I had only glanced at before and keeping half an eye on the screen. The commercial break came and went, and even when the newscaster said something about a demonstration at a meeting addressed by the Defence Minister I didn't immediately connect it with what I had seen earlier. Indeed, I might have missed the report altogether if I hadn't finished the paper just then and put it aside. But once I saw the first few seconds, I watched with all the interest one takes in reports of events one has witnessed.

Skilful camera work and editing, while they didn't exactly convey a false impression, nevertheless made the scenes seem more dramatic than they had done at the time. Or so I thought at first. Then I realized that some of them had been recorded after I walked on: the doors opening while the police struggled to hold back the demonstrators and a small group emerging.

I had seen pictures of Gerald Sapsed in the papers and on television often enough to recognize him now—a youngish man, stockily built, with smooth dark hair brushed across his head and springing out over his ears, and bland, politician's features. Hardly a military figure. But I knew he had the reputation of being aggressive in debate, and they said his political opponents respected him.

A woman, presumably Mrs. Sapsed, was on his left. She was blonde and good looking in a lean, greyhound way. A younger man, fair haired and worried looking, was behind them, and another man, older and with the look of a prosperous businessman, brought up the rear. For a moment they hesitated in the doorway, facing the crowd, then, with as much dignity as they could manage, they walked rather hurriedly to a large car drawn up by the kerb. You could see the flashes from the photographers, but the shouts were lost in the pandemonium. A policeman was pushed or knocked to the ground, and his helmet rolled away.

"Seven people were hurt, four of them policemen, and

there were six arrests," the newscaster reported. "A little later, Norman Widdiford spoke to Mr. and Mrs. Sapsed."

He must have been waiting for them when they reached home, for they were getting out of the same car, with a pleasant old whitewashed house in the background. Because he had planned it that way, or simply because the car drew up on that side of him, the reporter approached Mrs. Sapsed first, before her husband had time to walk round the car to join her. Afterwards I wondered if he had done it deliberately. Seeing him, she waited, smiling.

"You must be shaken after what happened this evening, Mrs. Sapsed," he suggested.

"Certainly not. Why should I be? One really can't allow oneself to be intimidated by that sort of rabble." Her voice was rather high pitched and imperious. "What you saw this evening was typical of far too many people here. Especially the students of course."

For a brief moment Sapsed's face appeared within shot looking shocked and angry. But Widdiford wasn't going to leave Mrs. Sapsed yet.

"They seem to think they can live off the rest of us while they do nothing useful, just make trouble," she went on. "It's a great pity the media give them so much publicity; it's just what they want. You only have to look at the layabouts at the Polytechnic; most of them are Left-wing agitators."

She stopped, and after a moment's hesitation while he waited to see if she would say anything more, Widdiford turned to her husband. "Have you anything to add to what Mrs. Sapsed has said, sir?"

The minister looked grim. "My wife is understandably a little distraught," he said.

She didn't look distraught, I reflected. Rather, she seemed to be fully in control of herself and to know exactly what she was saying. Undiplomatic, exaggerated, even vicious, it might have been, but it was what she meant. Perhaps she saw the interview as an opportunity to lash back at the crowd who had humiliated her, and she was relishing it. Clearly Sapsed wasn't; he looked far more disturbed than his wife.

"Naturally everybody has a right to his or her opinions and to express them, so long as it's done in a reasonable way," he said smoothly. "Unfortunately, I'm afraid a small minority of the people you saw tonight allowed themselves to be rather carried away. It's a great pity, but that's part of the price you've got to pay if you're going to have free speech."

The camera turned back to the reporter. "Thank you, Mr. Sapsed. This is Norman Widdiford at Lemsfield for 'News at Ten.'"

I watched the rest of the programme, switched off and went to bed.

THREE

Breakfast at the Lamb was a sedately leisured meal. The heavy old cutlery might be losing its plating and the elderly waitresses move slowly and arthritically between the tables, but the dining-room when I entered it at ten past eight had a dignity it hadn't possessed the previous evening. A slightly seedy dignity, perhaps, but an air of good living and good manners for all that. The waitress who came to take my order must have been at least sixty-five, with grey hair and kind, weak eyes behind her glasses. I asked her for orange juice, a kipper, toast and coffee, and opened my *Telegraph*.

Already my first disappointment at not getting Bill Sale's job was fading and I was more or less reconciled to staying with the Department for the next few months. It wasn't as if I disliked the work, so why should I feel this slightly resentful dissatisfaction? I knew why all right: because something else had been dangled in front of me, only to be snatched away again.

By the time I reached the bank it was past nine and the rest of the team were already there. Trevor reported that the entry drill hadn't been carried out in accordance with instructions and that some cash had been left in one of the tills overnight. I sighed. It was probably the first time it had happened for months, years even, but it would have to go on the report. If they hadn't the sense to take more care during an inspection, they deserved it.

I was going to start reviewing the advances this morning.

Arming myself with the computer centre's print-out of all the loans and overdrafts at the branch and the record cards for the customers whose names started with A, B and C, I took myself off to the staff-room.

For the next hour or so I worked steadily, undisturbed. Leaving the small advances for Ben to deal with, I tried to assess from the notes on the cards the soundness of the bigger lendings and if any of them were likely to cause problems, either because they had been injudicious in the first place or the customers' circumstances had changed. Even without his initial in the margin it would have been easy to tell which notes were Waites'; his personality came through in the slightly preachy wording. But by the end of that first hour I had found none of his advances that called for comment. It wasn't so much that he possessed a flair for lending as that he was so cautious there was practically no chance of anything going wrong.

Caroline Bedford's notes were brief to the point of curtness, but they told anyone reading them all he needed to know. Moreover, I guessed she had the flair Waites lacked: the ability to size up a case and make the right decision.

Soon after ten, people started coming for their coffee. The women chattered about their husbands and boy friends and holidays, the men about sport; none of them took much notice of me beyond a friendly hallo. Miss Bedford came just before eleven. I noticed that, although she answered pleasantly enough when anybody spoke to her directly, she showed no inclination to join in the conversation, and I gained the impression of a person to whom small talk didn't come easily and who was, perhaps, rather uncomfortably aware of her intellectual superiority. Or perhaps it was just that she was a good deal older than the others who were in the room then. Not so much aloof as reserved. And not shy.

Waites didn't come to the staff-room. His coffee was taken

down to his room by the messenger, a lugubrious Welshman named Bill Old. Probably the rest of the staff preferred it that way.

Inevitably some of the talk was about the previous evening's demonstration. Few of the girls cared much about the political issues, but they had been excited seeing their town and people they knew on the news. One of them had a boy friend at the Polytechnic, but there was little sympathy for the demonstrators. Nevertheless, most of them resented what Mrs. Sapsed had said, seeing it as a slur on the town and thus, indirectly, on them.

"I didn't think she'd talk like that," a fair girl who was a cashier remarked. "She's always friendly when she comes in."

"She was shaken," an older woman commented. "Wouldn't you have been?"

"I don't care if she was; she shouldn't have said those things," a third said. "There were only a few who made any trouble—and they weren't all students."

"I think she was right," the older one maintained.

"You would, Jenny." There was no malice in the fair girl's tone.

"He didn't like it, did he?" the third one put in, sounding almost pleased, like somebody relating the details of a stranger's misfortunes. "You could see he didn't."

I glanced at Caroline Bedford sitting near the end of one of the settees. She hadn't looked up, but I noticed that her fingers had stopped turning the pages of the magazine she was holding and I had the feeling she was waiting, tense, for what might be said next. Then one of the other girls said something about a customer being abusive to her on the telephone, and almost visibly she relaxed. I told myself I must have been mistaken, but nevertheless my curiosity was aroused.

For the rest of the day, I concentrated on the advances. The branch had a good cross-section of business: companies with factories on the industrial estates, farmers, shopkeepers, professional firms and private individuals. There were a handful of potentially troublesome lendings, but they were fewer than might have been expected in a branch like Lemsfield; a manager soon acquires a reputation for being a willing or a reluctant lender, and it was unlikely many dubious business propositions came Waites' way.

Just before five I called it a day. Collecting my papers together, I put them in my briefcase and carried the record cards downstairs to replace them in their filing-cabinet. Ben and Trevor were coming up from the strong-room. They were yawning—strong-rooms were generally pretty airless places, especially when they were underground, and today it was hot again.

"Okay?" I enquired.

They nodded. "There's not much so far," Trevor reported.

It was normal for Inspection teams to leave before the branch staffs. For one thing, they often had considerable distances to travel, and for another, branches were glad to have them out of the way while they were finishing off the day's work. We rounded up the others, who were talking to the securities clerks, said goodbye and departed, the others to drive home, I to return to the lonely comforts of the Lamb.

Vickie, the receptionist, was behind her desk when I walked in. She handed me my key, and I bought a copy of the local paper. The front page was devoted almost exclusively to coverage of the previous evening's events. I glanced at the editorial. Its comments on Mrs. Sapsed's televized remarks were regretful, rather than critical: relations between the town and the Polytechnic had always been good, and the *Star* trusted they would not be impaired by words spoken under great stress or the violent behaviour of a small number of hooligans which was deplored as much by most students as it was by the townspeople. It was pretty predictable stuff.

One or two of the letters were less restrained. You could hardly blame Sapsed's political opponents for making the most of his wife's gaffe, I supposed, but there were two letters from people who claimed they had voted for him at the last election but were now so angered by her comments they would never do so again. The affair looked like becoming a local *cause célèbre* until something else came along to capture the headlines and distract the public's attention.

Folding the paper, I went to telephone Laura. Although I could tell she was still very worried about her mother, she didn't sound as depressed as I had been afraid she would; the tests were completed, but the results wouldn't be known for a day or two. She felt frustrated. There wasn't much she could do, but she didn't like to leave.

"I think I'll come home on Friday," she said.

I left it to her; I wanted her back, but I wasn't going to try to persuade her.

As I finished dinner it began to rain, a heavy, thundery shower that sent people scurrying for shelter and spray sluicing from the wheels of passing traffic. I abandoned the idea of going for a walk, and as I didn't fancy sitting in my bedroom watching television, retreated to the bar. It was busier than the previous evening, and I was surprised to see Waites there with a middle-aged couple and a man about my age whom I was pretty sure I had seen before but couldn't remember where. The older man was running to a paunch and wore heavy-rimmed glasses. The woman was a well-preserved forty-five or so with her hair streaked blonde, a trim figure and a good deal of makeup. Her clothes were smart and looked expensive.

Waites was buying their drinks and making rather a lot of it. I hoped he wouldn't turn and see me waiting at the bar, but I couldn't very well walk out. Then he did and I saw the surprise show for a second in his cold blue eyes.

"Good evening, Mr. Grierson," he said quite cordially. "Are you staying here?"

I told him I was, thinking uncomfortably that he would probably feel obliged to offer to buy me a drink, and if he did I couldn't refuse without appearing rude, although we would both be happier if I did.

"They're looking after you, I hope?" From his tone he might have owned the place. Perhaps the people who did were his customers, and if I said they weren't he would mention it to them.

"Very, thank you," I answered.

"Are you on your own?"

"Yes."

"Won't you join us, then?"

He didn't want me tagging on to his little group any more than I wanted to join them. But it would be churlish to decline when he was trying to be friendly.

"Thank you," I said.

"What can I get you to drink?"

I saw the others were drinking shorts and asked if I could have a bitter.

"Certainly you can, Mr. Grierson." He smiled, and it occurred to me that he wanted to be like other people and for them to like him, but he didn't know how. His trouble was that he lacked warmth or any real interest in them—and it showed. I knew nobody else in the Bank below the general managers who would have called me "Mr. Grierson" except ironically. And Waites wasn't being ironic.

I had expected him to buy me a half, not from meanness but because he would consider it more appropriate, pints being for pubs and rugger clubs, but he didn't.

"I envy you," he told me, watching me pick up the pint

glass. "I would rather drink beer, but the doctor won't let me."

I was a little ashamed of my too facile judgement.

He introduced me to the others. The couple's name was Henderson; I gathered he was the boss of a company which banked at the branch and she was vice-chairman of the local Conservative Association. The younger man was Martyn Carthy—"Martyn with a 'y,' " Mrs. Henderson informed me with a smile. He was Gerald Sapsed's agent. That, of course, was where I had seen him before, on television last night, coming out of the civic hall behind the minister. He had a roundish face and a harassed look.

Apparently they had been in the middle of a conversation when I appeared, and they soon reverted to it.

"You've got to make allowances, Edna," Henderson protested. "Good lord, look what she'd gone through."

"It's going to cost him votes next time," Mrs. Henderson insisted. "I'm right, aren't I, Martyn?"

"I hope not," Carthy said diffidently.

"I am. You know I am. And Gerald has enough on his mind just now. I can't imagine what she was thinking about, lashing out like that."

"She's a damned good member's wife," Henderson objected.

"Oh, everybody likes her, I grant you that. I like her myself."

"Probably she's just bored."

"She can't be bored."

Henderson laughed comfortably.

"It's no good your laughing, George, she mustn't. Gerald only got in by nine hundred-odd last time, and she's upset a lot of people who voted for him. He might very well lose the seat."

"It could be serious," Carthy admitted, looking solemn.

"Hooey. There won't be an election for another two years at least; people will have forgotten all about it by then."

"Not if she keeps on doing that sort of thing," Mrs. Henderson retorted. "Last night wasn't the first time."

"You think she's all right anyway, don't you, Martyn?" her husband asked, as if he was trying to put the conversation on a lighter plane.

But the agent looked embarrassed. He was a paid official; he didn't like being asked to express an opinion about the Member's wife, I thought.

"Oh, we all know Martyn thinks she's wonderful," Mrs. Henderson agreed, laughing good humouredly but at the same time sounding mildly exasperated.

"How long do you expect to be with us?" Waites asked me. Perhaps he wasn't as interested as the others in politics. Or thought I wouldn't be.

"I hope we shall be finished by the end of next week," I told him.

He nodded rather portentously and proceeded to tell a long and boring anecdote about an inspection at a branch when he was a securities clerk there. He had just finished it when Carthy muttered, "Oh, God!" with so much feeling I turned, startled. I couldn't believe it had been a comment on Waites' story.

He was looking towards the door. Hillyer, the man I had met here last night, had come in and was leaning against the bar.

"It's Peter," Edna Henderson said. It was impossible to tell from her tone whether she was surprised, pleased or annoyed.

"Half pissed as usual," her husband commented.

"Well, it's half-past eight," Carthy observed, a sting in his voice. There was a momentary silence. "I'd better be going. I promised to look in at the Kingsridge school. Thank you for the drink, Mr. Waites."

Waites smiled benevolently. I wondered if I was right and Carthy's decision to leave had been prompted by Hillyer's arrival.

"He can't stand Peter," Mrs. Henderson observed when he had gone. "Poor Martyn."

"I don't blame him," her husband told her. "Hillyer's a useless bastard. He owes money all over the place, and most of the time he's drunk. Have you seen that place of his?"

"I met him last night," I said. "He button-holed me in here. Who is he?"

"He farms out at Hensbourn Green," Henderson answered. "His father had a place Aylesbury way somewhere but it went to the brother. Hillyer rents his farm from the Church Commissioners or somebody."

Waites started talking about cricket. The way he did it made me wonder if Hillyer was one of his customers and the conversation was embarrassing him. Henderson bought another round and said something about changes in Lemsfield. I gathered that some of the old residents still resented the New Town. It had been there over twenty years, but they still looked back nostalgically to the days when Lemsfield had been a market town with a population of twelve thousand, very little industry and no supermarkets. I asked what people thought about the Polytechnic and was slightly surprised when Mrs. Henderson told me that most of them approved of it. Several of their friends had sons or daughters who were students there.

"That's why Rosemary was so stupid saying all those things," she observed.

Soon after that, Waites departed, declining to let me buy him a drink, and the Hendersons followed him almost immediately. I decided I might as well have another half to keep me company while I tried to solve the crossword in that morning's *Telegraph*, and went up to the bar.

Hillyer was talking to a couple there. If he had been half-drunk when he came in he had progressed since then. His speech was slurred, and the woman was openly laughing at him. I bought my drink, took it over to one of the tables and tried to concentrate on the crossword, without much success. In the end I gave up and went up to my room to watch the BBC news.

The crisis in NATO was worsening. For the first time in the history of the alliance, according to the commentator, there was a real risk of its disintegrating. If it did, and the Americans withdrew their troops from the Continent, Western Europe would be virtually defenceless in the face of any threats from the East. At present the Russian leaders were playing it very cool, no doubt because they calculated that the surest way of healing the breach was for them to adopt a threatening posture. Conversely, if they presented an image of peaceful reason, the Allies could be left to split up into impotent factions. He detailed the comparative forces on each side of the Iron Curtain. It wasn't pleasant viewing, but apart from the politicians and the journalists nobody seemed to be worrying much. I hadn't heard anybody mention NATO since the fracas outside the civic hall, and I felt slightly guilty at being more concerned with the prospects for the cricket season.

When the news ended, I switched off and read for an hour.

FOUR

The inspection proceeded smoothly and without problems. The branch was well managed, rules were observed, security was good and morale reasonable; there was little that called for any adverse comment. The manager might be nominally responsible, but the smooth running of a branch depended on the sub-manager, and Waites was fortunate in Harry Roche; he himself took little interest in the day-to-day routine.

Caroline Bedford did; she involved herself a good deal. Together she and Harry made a good team: she possessed insight and judgement, he had the organizing ability and the rapport with the younger members of the staff to get things done.

The next day, there were more letters in the *Star*. It seemed to me it was a lot of fuss to make over a woman's outburst in a moment of stress, but there was no doubt Rosemary Sapsed had stirred up a hornet's nest, and I wondered if she regretted her words now.

That evening something occurred which didn't seem very sinister at the time but which later was to appear much more significant. Mrs. Sapsed had parked her car in a side-street near the Ridings while she visited the Conservative office. She was gone only ten or fifteen minutes, but that was long enough for somebody to spray paint obscenities along one side. Across the bonnet was the message "POLY RULES O K?"

I heard about it when a customer came into the bar at the Lamb just before nine o'clock. Soon everybody there knew.

Generally, I gathered, they were on her side, and it seemed that, despite her televised criticisms of the town, she was still well liked.

Hillyer didn't come into the Lamb that evening, but Martyn Carthy put in an appearance about nine forty-five. He was alone and we had a drink together. Without other people there, he talked more freely than he had done in front of Waites and the Hendersons, but he still struck me as a strangely uncertain man for his job. However, when he talked about it, or politics in general, he became a different person, still likeable but more confident and self-assured.

He told me he had been born and brought up in Somerset, gone to a grammar school and, his father insisting he started "proper work," taken his four A-levels into an accountant's office instead of going on to university. I gathered his father had been a pretty forceful character, which possibly explained Carthy's diffidence. Perhaps his lack of confidence outside his job extended to women, for he was a bachelor.

The next day, I continued work on the advances, and by coffee-time I had reached the S's. The last card had been John Reginald Samson's, and there was no very good reason why, when I picked up the next and saw it was headed "SAPSED Gerald Baillie," I should feel a slight sense of shock. Yet I did. I had heard his name so often since coming to Lemsfield, and the other morning at coffee one of the cashiers had talked about his wife coming into the bank, but nobody had said he was a customer.

He had transferred his accounts from a London branch three years ago, soon after he was adopted as the prospective candidate. Prior to that, he had been the member for a constituency which had disappeared in a welter of boundary changes, and a junior minister. Eighteen months ago he had been granted a loan of £7,000 to help pay for work he was having done to his house; since then the loan had been increased twice, and now, even after the monthly repayments, it still stood at £9,140. In addition, although there was no arrangement for an overdraft and no limit had been marked, his current account was overdrawn £4,821. When the loan was first taken, he had charged some shares as security, but the last of them had been released six months ago and now both advances were unsecured.

The original advance had been agreed to by Caroline Bedford, and apparently she had handled the accounts ever since. I found that a little surprising; I would have expected Waites to want to deal with the local Conservative MP. Especially when he was a Cabinet Minister. Had he foreseen he would be unable to agree to help Sapsed as much as the latter wanted and passed the responsibility on to Miss Bedford? If she granted the loan, he could disclaim immediate responsibility afterwards. I had heard of managers who did that. Would Waites?

Whatever the reason for Miss Bedford's handling the accounts, why hadn't she taken a charge over the house? It was the obvious security, as the advance was to finance work on it. Had Sapsed or his wife refused?

I went back to the first notes on the record card. They had been made by Harry Roche's predecessor when Sapsed wanted to change his car and he had marked an overdraft limit of £800 for six months. The overdraft had been cleared in four.

There were no details of the work for which the latest loan had been needed, nor was there any record of Sapsed's producing estimates or receipted accounts. Moreover, apart from a laconic "Further work to be done to house," there was no explanation for the subsequent increases, while the only references to the overdraft were brief notes on the lines of "Have spoken to customer and he will correct the position" and "Increase caused by expenses incurred in connection with his work." It seemed clear Sapsed was living beyond his means and, however safe the advances might be in the long run, I was surprised Miss Bedford had dealt with them so casually. Unless I had badly misjudged her, it was out of character.

Also, they were outside the branch's discretion. Every branch had a limit up to which the manager could lend to a customer; any advance beyond that figure had to be sanctioned by district office. Different advances to the same customer were lumped together. Sapsed's borrowings had been outside the branch's discretion for five months and there was nothing on his record card to show they had been reported. That was both serious and puzzling.

I made some notes and put the card aside with the others to be discussed with Waites. Quite often, a lending which appeared unsatisfactory to an outsider looked very different when you knew all the facts—although they should be recorded on the card.

If it had been anyone else's account I would probably have forgotten about it until I talked to Waites. As it was, my curiosity was aroused. What sort of man was the Minister? I had seen him occasionally on television and read odd items about him in the papers, but I knew nothing about him as a person. On Monday night on television, running the gauntlet of the demonstrators outside the civic hall, he had looked undignified, almost ridiculous. Something in me, as in most people, I suspected, enjoyed seeing a public figure cut down to size, but perhaps by diminishing them we diminished ourselves. Wouldn't anyone in Sapsed's situation then have looked like that? The picture I had seen was probably as false as his smooth, dark-suited public persona. Or was that image the real man? Surely not. He must have ability and other qualities to have reached his present position. Anyway, what difference did it make? He spent too much.

I turned to the next card.

"G. B. Sapsed," I said.

"He sees Miss Bedford."

Had I imagined a slight complacency in Waites' tone? If so, there could be a dozen reasons for it, none of them admirable.

"They seem pretty generous lendings," I suggested mildly.

There was a long silence. Waites picked up his pipe and tapped it out slowly and deliberately on his heavy ash-tray. His long, bloodhound's face was expressionless. Then he observed heavily, "When you have been in the bank as long as I have you will find that advances which may appear generous, as you call it, are sometimes sound banking. It's all a matter of judgement—and that comes only with experience."

Patronizing sod, I thought. I wondered who had given Waites the idea he was good at dealing with people; his habit of stopping in mid-sentence for several seconds, then finishing with a sententious banality was calculated to drive any normal person up the wall in ten minutes. If he was the same at home, God help his family! And anyway, what he had said was irrelevant: Caroline Bedford had been in the bank less time than I had. He was just getting at me.

There had been eleven advances about which I had had reservations, five of them his. He had satisfied me I could forget two, which left three to go in the report. As for the other six, he had made it clear I must talk to Miss Bedford about them. Which was fair enough; it was the way he said it that irritated me.

"I'll talk to Miss Bedford about the others," I told him, thinking that experience, useful though it undoubtedly was, had little to do with the basic rules of banking I had had drummed into me by my old manager up North. Waites was one of those people who see age as a merit in itself, an unanswerable assertion.

"Yes, do," he agreed with all the self-satisfaction of one who has scored a point.

Caroline Bedford was in her room, dictating letters into a machine. When I asked if she could spare me a few minutes she said, "Yes," in her cool voice and put down the microphone. Today she was wearing a slim cream dress with narrow horizontal stripes and a black belt, and she looked almost lost in the big swivel chair.

"I've been going through the advances," I explained. "There aren't many."

Had she tensed slightly? If she had, it didn't necessarily mean anything; even the most experienced managers sometimes lost a little of their composure when their lendings were scrutinized.

We soon disposed of the first five accounts; three would have to be reported, but it was unlikely the bank would lose any money. I had kept Sapsed's to the last.

"G. B. Sapsed," I said for the second time in the last quarter of an hour.

I was sure about the tenseness now; she had been expecting this, waiting for it. Perhaps even dreading it. But she still wasn't quite prepared.

"He'll be all right," she said coolly. "You know who he is, don't you?"

"Yes."

"We're getting monthly reductions in the loan and he's selling shares to repay the overdraft."

"The loan has had to be increased twice. Did you see any estimates or receipts?"

"I didn't consider it necessary with somebody of his standing."

"It's a good practice."

Something flashed behind her cool grey eyes. "That's the sort of remark inspectors usually make."

I knew then she had made up her mind to dislike me, and I was sorrier about it than I would have expected.

"I can't see it's been reported," I told her. "It's been outside the branch discretion for some time."

"It's been reported and sanctioned."

"Can you let me see the report?"

She frowned. "It's in the file."

"I couldn't find it."

"Then either it's been mis-sorted or it was overlooked. I'm sorry."

She was annoyed with me, but more with herself. Failure to report an excess wouldn't be regarded as too serious if it was a single instance and clearly an oversight, but this had gone on for months. She knew she could expect a reprimand from district office and she didn't like it; she was a proud young woman.

"If I were you, I'd report it now," I told her. There was nothing to be gained by my making too much of it; she knew Sapsed's would be one of the advances I would have to report and if she got in first, sufficiently contrite, it would help. District office might make disapproving noises, but they must think highly of her, there weren't many girl a/m's her age, and they would sanction the advances in the end. They had little choice, short of insisting they were called in—and they would hardly do that when the customer was a Cabinet Minister.

"What sort of man is he?" I asked.

"In what way?"

"As a person."

"Oh, quite pleasant."

"Not a charlatan?"

"No."

"Does he come in often?"

"No, hardly ever."

"That's all, then," I said. "Thank you."

I had reached the door when she asked casually, "How long will you be here?"

Everybody wanted us to go, I thought. If it went on, I'd start becoming paranoid about it. "Another ten days, I should think," I answered.

She picked up the microphone and started dictating again without saying anything more.

Outside, in the main office, I went to the securities section and found the register which contained the S's. The branch had held share certificates for Sapsed in the past, but when the charge over them was released, the shares had been sold and now there were none left. So Caroline Bedford hadn't checked. She had taken it for granted that an advance to Sapsed was safe and she could dispense with both security and taking the normal precautions. True, he might have certificates somewhere else, but the fact that the others had been sold through the Bank and not outside brokers suggested he hadn't. So where were the shares he intended selling to repay his overdraft?

On an impulse I went up to the machine-room and for the second time extracted his ledger sheets from the tray. I made a list of the dates when the largest cheques had been debited and asked the supervisor to get one of her staff to find them and bring them to me in the staff-room.

She came after ten minutes. All but one of the cheques were payable to "Cash." It looked as if Sapsed had been helping whoever did the work on his house to avoid paying tax.

FIVE

They still brought morning tea to your room at the Lamb; there was none of the staff-saving make-it-yourself-on-a-machine apology for service. The maid who came to my room was young, foreign and very plain. The next morning, exactly three minutes late, she tapped on my door, waited for me to call, "Come in," and when I did, carried in my tray with a copy of the *Daily Telegraph* balanced beside the tea-things.

"Good morning, sir." She had adenoids, and they added to her difficulty in speaking English.

"Good morning," I said. I had been awake for a quarter of an hour, listening to the record programme on the radio and debating whether to get up before my tea came or afterwards. Afterwards had won.

The girl put down the tray, scrupulously avoiding looking at me, and retreated. The door closed behind her. I poured a cup of tea and unfolded the paper to read it while the tea cooled.

The headline was on the front page: "CABINET MINISTER'S WIFE FOUND DEAD. Mrs. Gerald Sapsed Murdered."

I stared at it, not believing. Although I had never met her, had seen her only once on television, I had heard so much about her and her husband since I came to Lemsfield that, absurdly, her death seemed to affect me personally. I started reading the report.

It seemed that yesterday evening, after Sapsed had left to drive to Westminster, his wife had taken her dogs for a walk.

Just before ten, she had told their French *au pair* she wouldn't
be gone long, walked across the lawn and the meadow beyond
and entered a small wood which bordered their land on the
west. A quarter of an hour later the dogs had returned without
her. They had seemed distressed and restless, but Monique
Chabrier, the *au pair*, had assumed that was because their
mistress had stopped to talk to somebody and left them to
find their own way home. It had happened before. However,
when Mrs. Sapsed still hadn't returned an hour later, the girl
became worried and set out to look for her.

She had found the body at the foot of a tree, the dog's leads
still clutched in the dead woman's hand. She had been
stabbed three times; two of the wounds had penetrated her
heart and the third her left lung, killing her almost immediately. The weapon hadn't been found.

So much was in the report. On an inside page, "Peterbor-
ough's" column contained a tribute to the dead woman's work
in the constituency and her charm and popularity. Before his
death her father had been the chairman of several companies,
including one of Britain's biggest insurance groups. That suggested a monied background or, at least, comparative afflu-
ence. Sapsed had been an economics lecturer at a red-brick
university; had he been relying on his wife's money when he
lived so far beyond his means? Perhaps there had been some
understanding between them.

I put down the paper, gulped some tea and climbed out of
bed. The murder was shocking, and the victim had been a
customer of the Bank's, but I didn't see that her death would
affect me personally.

Which showed how mistaken I could be.

To mark the gravity of the occasion, Waites had arrived at
the bank early, and when I got there he was in his room with
Miss Bedford. I suspected he would be in his element today,
trotting out his stock of clichés.

Understandably, the staff were full of the murder. Although they were distressed by what had happened, they would hardly have been human if they hadn't felt a slightly shame-faced excitement.

"Did she come in often?" I asked Stephanie Fortune, the first cashier.

"Every week or two," she answered. "She used to cash her cheques. And she had a deed-box she used to have out some-times."

She probably kept her jewellery in it; a woman in her position would have to attend a good many formal affairs.

Caroline Bedford came into the main office looking slightly strained and less poised than usual. She stopped by the securities desk and I heard her say to Hodgson, the senior clerk, "Mr. Waites has had a call from Mrs. Sapsed's solicitors; they can't find her will."

"Did she leave one?" Hodgson asked.

"Yes. The Bank's the executor."

That possibility hadn't occurred to me, but I couldn't see it changed the situation; Executor and Trustee Department would handle everything with her solicitor and, except indi-rectly, the branch would hardly be involved. But it was strange her will wasn't here; it was the normal procedure, when the Bank was appointed, for the customer's branch to hold the will. Mrs. Sapsed must have had her own reasons for wanting to keep it somewhere else.

"It may be in her deed-box," Caroline Bedford said. "Colin Bates is coming over this morning to open it; he's meeting Mr. Sapsed and her solicitor here. They'll be here at eleven; make sure it's ready then, will you, Gordon?"

Colin Bates was the assistant manager at E & T's regional office, but I wondered why Sapsed wanted to be there. Pre-sumably he had expressed a wish to be.

Miss Bedford looked round, said briskly, "All right, let's get on with it," and went off towards her room. For some reason I felt guilty—as if she had caught me wasting time.

It seemed to be taken for granted I should be present when the box was opened. Quite why Inspection should be represented, I couldn't see. After all, if the will was there, so well and good; if it wasn't, that would be Executor & Trustee's problem. Perhaps, I thought, Waites regarded me as a sort of insurance, to take responsibility off his shoulders if anything went wrong. But why should it?

Sapsed arrived with the solicitor at one minute past eleven. Seen at close quarters, he was slimmer, shrewder and less bland than he appeared on television—though the last could have been due to the circumstances. So could my sudden unexpected impression of vulnerability. He was wearing a dark suit and looked as if he hadn't slept much last night. When he spoke it was quietly and pleasantly.

The solicitor was a tall, grey-haired man of about sixty named Wheatley, who looked as if, quite consciously, he did all he could to look and sound like the archetypal family lawyer; he was thin, stooped and wore gold-rimmed glasses a shade too far down his rather long, thin nose to gain much benefit from them. His sparse hair was brushed carefully across his scalp, and despite the heat he wore a grey pin-stripe, three-piece suit. Colin Bates arrived on their heels, full of apologies. He was Wheatley's opposite in nearly every way, young, stocky and vaguely untidy, but he was nobody's fool.

Waites expressed our horror and sympathy. I had no doubt he was sincere; it was his misfortune that he made the sentiments sound synthetic. He introduced Miss Bedford and Bates, explained I was one of the Bank's inspectors there on a routine visit and asked the assistant manager to fetch the deed-box.

Sapsed looked forbearing, and I reflected angrily that

Waites was staging this macabre pantomime for his own grati-
fication. It was unnecessary; Bates and the solicitor could have
taken the box to the waiting-room and opened it there with or
without Sapsed's presence.

Then Miss Bedford returned carrying an ordinary, medium-
sized black deed-box, obviously not new but not scratched or
dented. From the way she handled it, it contained nothing
very heavy. She put it down on Waites' desk and stepped
back. Sapsed produced a key from his pocket and handed it to
the lawyer.

There was nothing inherently dramatic in what was happening, yet I was conscious of a new tenseness in the atmosphere. Nor was I alone; I could see from their faces that the
others felt it too. All except the solicitor. The room faced east,
and that part of it where the rest of us were standing was
already in semi-shadow; only Wheatley and the box were in
the full light of the sun streaming in at the corner of the
window, and that enhanced the theatrical effect.

Bates was nearest to him, with Sapsed on his right and
Waites behind him. Caroline Bedford was on Bates' other
side, nearest to me. As Wheatley inserted the key in the lock
and turned it, I could have sworn we all leaned forward. I had
a sudden, insane notion that he was opening a coffin and
hardly dared watch. The next moment I nearly burst out
laughing; the box appeared to be filled with identical white
envelopes. A layer of them, arranged in neat rows, took up the
whole visible surface.

Then somebody breathed, "Oh, God!" It was Sapsed. I
looked across at him and was startled to see that he appeared
to be almost overcome by shock. He was staring at the box as
though it exerted some dreadful fascination and he couldn't
take his eyes off it.

Wheatley had his back to the rest of us, and the others
were watching him, so that they couldn't see Sapsed's face.

The solicitor picked up one of the envelopes and studied it. The flap was open. He looked inside it, and an expression of mild surprise, almost distaste, crossed his lean, fastidious features.

"It seems to contain ten-pound notes," he commented.

I glanced again at Sapsed. Something about him gave me the impression that he was having to call on all his reserves of self-control to appear calm. I looked away. Near me, Caroline Bedford had gone very pale, and for a moment I thought she was going to faint. Then, with a visible effort, she pulled herself together. I saw her glance briefly at Sapsed, then back at the box.

Wheatley was looking in the other envelopes. "There seems to be money in all of them," he said. "It must amount to a considerable sum. Perhaps, Mr. Bates . . ."

"Yes, of course." Colin Bates looked less concerned than anyone there, with the possible exception of Waites. "I'll get one of the cashiers to count it and pay it in to a suspense account for the time being." He turned to Waites.

"Certainly," the manager agreed.

There were two layers of envelopes, fourteen in all. Wheatley stacked them in two tidy little piles on the desk. Under them were several jewel cases and some more envelopes, but these were larger and marked clearly with details of their contents. One of them had the single word "WILL" printed on it in very black gothic letters. The lawyer handed it to Bates, replaced the other things in the box and, when he had locked it, handed him the key, too. Bates put it in his briefcase and slit the end of the envelope.

I watched him as he scanned the two typewritten pages quickly, and I saw his sudden frown of surprise, almost shock. Sapsed had regained his composure and seemed barely interested in what was happening; he probably knew the contents of the will already.

Bates refolded it, slid it back into the envelope and put it away in his case. "There are no specific instructions regarding the funeral or cremation," he said quietly.

In any case, I reflected, that would have to be postponed until after the inquest. Hadn't I heard somewhere that where the dead person had been murdered the body remained the property of the State for ever? It seemed macabre, but who else should one's body belong to? Anyway, I'd probably got it wrong.

"Er, thank you, Mr. Waites." Wheatley picked up the two piles of envelopes. "If you and Mr. Bates would be kind enough to have someone deal with these?"

Caroline Bedford seemed to come back to life. "I will," she volunteered in a flat voice, taking them from him.

"Let me help," I told her. For her protection they should be in two people's charge; according to the lawyer, they contained a substantial sum, and if she had it in her sole keeping, even for a few minutes, and someone suggested later there had been more in the box than she had paid in, it would be very difficult to refute the charge. It might be unlikely, but unlikely things happened. The motto of Inspection might have been "Better Safe Than Sorry," I thought.

For a moment it seemed she was going to argue that she didn't need my help, but then she let me take half the envelopes and we walked out of the room, watched in silence by the others.

"Are you all right?" I asked her as we walked along the corridor to the main office and round behind the counter.

"Yes, of course. Why?" Her tone was sharp.

"You looked as if you were going to pass out in there."

"Rubbish." As if it were an afterthought, she added, "It was very stuffy."

It hadn't been that stuffy, I reflected. Warm, yes, but Waites had had the window open, and by this time people were more or less accustomed to the heat. Still, it was none of my business.

The girl at the end till was free. We handed over the envelopes and watched while she counted the contents twice. All the cash was in ten-pound notes, and it totalled £9,500. The girl made out a credit slip, stamped and initialled both it and the counterfoil and gave the latter to Miss Bedford. She took it and walked away, back in the direction of the manager's room.

On an impulse, not knowing why I did it, I picked up the bundle of empty envelopes and stuffed them in my jacket pocket. Perhaps it was merely an instinct for tidiness.

There was no point in my returning to Waites' room; I went to have a word with Ben and Trevor: then, because the staff-room was in use, settled down in the waiting-room to make some notes for my report. When I sat down, I felt the bulk of the envelopes in my pocket against the side of the chair. I took them out and was on the point of tossing them into the wastepaper-basket when something stopped me. I looked more closely at the top one. It was an ordinary white envelope approximately 8½ inches by 4½, neither cheaply flimsy nor expensively thick. The sort of envelope you could buy by the hundred in any stationer's. It bore no address and the paper was stained, as if it had been left in a dirty place at some time. The thin wad of notes it had contained had left their outline on the paper, and in the top left-hand corner "4/4/80" had been written in rather large, spiky figures. Presumably a date or a reference.

The flap of the envelope had been stuck down, then sealed more securely with a short strip of Sellotape; the surface of the paper was slightly damaged where the tape had been pulled off, leaving a cleaner strip about three quarters of an inch wide.

The other envelopes looked identical except that the figures on them were all different. Curious, I shoved them away in the bottom of my brief-case. It seemed strange to me that a woman like Rosemary Sapsed should hoard large sums of money in a deed-box. Had she been selling pieces of her jewellery? If so, it suggested either a need for money or a wish to reinvest the proceeds. So why put them somewhere where inflation would soon erode their value? No, more likely it was some form of tax dodge. That might explain Sapsed's shock when he saw the envelopes. A man in his position wouldn't want a scandal. Especially that sort.

But what did the dates, if they were dates, mean? And why had Caroline Bedford gone so pale when Wheatley opened the box? Perhaps the timing was only coincidence and there had been some feminine reason for her feeling faint. If so she might have blamed the atmosphere in the room to silence me.

I was curious, but I couldn't see any of it mattered and I had plenty of work to keep me busy. I took out a ball-point pen and started making notes.

SIX

From what the cashiers said, I gathered it was generally assumed in Lemsfield that Rosemary Sapsed's death had been a consequence of her televised comments about the local people and that she had been murdered by a fanatic whose resentment had exploded into deadly violence. It struck me as unlikely, but most murders were unlikely until they happened, and there were plenty of people about prepared to resort to violence for the most trivial reasons.

Doubtless there were plenty of rumours going around, but as an outsider I heard only a few of them—and nothing which suggested a more plausible motive for the crime. It seemed that the dead woman really had been liked by everybody.

But it was other things, only remotely connected with the murder, that intrigued me. First was Sapsed's involuntary "Oh, God!" when Wheatley opened the box and he saw the contents. What had caused that tortured exclamation? All he could see was the neat layer of envelopes; surely there was nothing alarming in that? Even the possibility that his wife had been evading tax hardly seemed to justify such horror.

Second was the expression I had seen on Caroline Bedford's face a few seconds later. It wasn't when she saw the envelopes; it was a second or two later, when the solicitor said they contained money. She had looked quickly at Sapsed, then away. As if the money had some significance for them both? Possibly. If so, it must have been something pretty serious to account for her nearly fainting.

Third were the envelopes themselves—or rather, their grubby condition. A woman like the Minister's wife, if she had wanted to keep money in her deed-box, would surely have used clean envelopes.

The more I pondered them, the more convinced I became that the three things were in some way connected. And without knowing why, I was uneasy. After all, a connection didn't mean any of them had anything to do with the murder—nor with the Bank. They were nothing to do with me and I could forget them.

Nevertheless my uneasiness persisted. Too vague to be real concern, it was more a gently nagging uncertainty. Just after twelve-thirty I told the others I wouldn't be having my usual snack with them and drove to the Lamb. Thursday was early closing day in Lemsfield, and although many of the shops in the New Town stayed open, the Old Town was already nearly deserted, preparing for its weekly siesta.

There were only a few cars in the car-park and not many more customers in the bar. By now Danny recognized me for a resident, and he asked. "The usual, sir?" ready to reach for a pint glass from the shelf as I walked in.

"Please," I told him, feeling the faint warmth of pleasure that comes from being recognized and accepted; the best salesmanship is based on flattery. "This murder's a nasty business."

"Yes indeed, sir." Danny gave the pump handle a second slow, steady pull. "She used to come in here sometimes. After meetings and that. A nice lady."

"Everybody seems to have liked her," I agreed, paying for the beer.

"They did, yes. She'll be missed. Used to take a great interest in local things, Mrs. Sapsed did."

"What's he like?" Why did I keep asking? Was I trying to

find somebody who would tell me she was a bitch and he an arrogant charlatan? I didn't know.

"Oh, he's a pleasant sort of man."

Danny looked along the bar to where two men and a woman were sitting half watching us, not talking. I knew they were listening to what we were saying; their faces, though blank, were somehow alert. Perhaps they disapproved of a stranger displaying any interest in local matters. Possibly they were more concerned with Danny's answers. He was uncomfortably aware of them, I was sure.

"I'll get some food," I told him.

A cold buffet was set out on a table in the window recess at the end of the room, joints of beef and ham and a turkey lording it over an array of salad ingredients. I drank enough of my beer to make it safe to carry and walked over. The chef, who had been leaning against a table, came to life and looked pleased to see a customer. I asked him for a beef salad. He carved three large slices of meat, dark on the outside, pink shading to red in the middle, and put together the salad as I selected it. I paid him and took the plate and my glass over to a table which was back near another window, in the lightest part of the room.

Folding my *Telegraph*, I propped it up against my beer-glass. But although I tried to concentrate on what I read, the two women at the next table were speaking so clearly it was impossible to ignore them.

"Some of those students look as if they'd be capable of almost anything," the one with her back to me observed. She had short dark hair plentifully streaked with grey and a rather petulant voice.

"Oh, I don't know." Her companion was younger, and as she leaned forward to stub out her cigarette her long grey-blonde hair swung forward, partly obscuring her face. I saw two eyes peering out boldly and a good deal of make-up. She saw me looking at her, and for a moment her eyes met mine and the corners of her mouth twitched slightly in the beginnings of a smile.

"Well, who else could it have been?"

The smile broadened in mischief. "They say most murders are committed by somebody in the family."

"Anne!"

The younger woman laughed, just too loudly. "It couldn't have been him, could it? He wasn't there."

"Just as well, if people are going to say things like that."

"Did you know her?"

"I'd spoken to her two or three times at meetings and wine and cheese parties and that. It's him I'm sorry for, having this to cope with on top of all the rest."

I chewed a mouthful of beef and tried to concentrate on the cricket reports. Then I heard the younger woman say, "There's Peter."

I looked up automatically. Hillyer had come in and was standing at the bar.

"I can't think how you can like him," the older woman commented.

Her companion laughed again. "Poor Peter. He's fun. And he's a lamb really."

"He owes money all over the town."

"So do lots of other people. Don't be a prig, Joan, for Heaven's sake."

"You'd feel the same if you had your own business."

"Yes, I expect I would. Does he owe you anything?"

"Me? I can't quite see him in one of my dresses."

"Lingerie for one of his girl friends?" Anne suggested. "Peter!"

Hillyer looked round and called, "Hello, Anne," in a tone which made me think he would have preferred her not to see him.

"Come and join us."

He came, not bothering to conceal his reluctance, carrying a glass of whisky, and sat down between them.

"What do you know, Peter?" Anne demanded.

"What about?"

"The murder, of course."

"I don't know anything except what I've read in the paper." He sounded almost truculent, like a schoolboy on the defensive.

"Oh, come on, Peter. You knew her much better than we did," Anne told him.

"Who says so?" Hillyer sounded less angry than alarmed, I thought.

"Well, didn't you? We hoped you'd be able to tell us what the police are doing and what they think."

"You did," the older woman told her tartly.

"I don't know anything." Hillyer gulped down the rest of his scotch and stood up, muttering something about having work to do. Then, without saying anything more, he walked out.

"Oh, dear," Anne said cheerfully.

"Really, Anne, I don't know how you can do it," her companion protested.

"Do what?"

"You know perfectly well. We'd better go too."

They collected their belongings and stood up.

"He did look awful, didn't he? Poor Peter." Anne looked over her shoulder at me and smiled. "Goodbye."

"Goodbye," I said, amused and a little startled.

When I got back to the Bank, I went straight to the waiting-room and rang Colin Bates. I explained I wanted to know the contents of Rosemary Sapsed's will, and he sounded a good deal less than pleased.

"Why not?" I asked. "After all, the branch will know as soon as you've got probate."

"Why do you want to know?"

"Sapsed's borrowing pretty heavily here. What's he likely to get?"

It was true, and it might have justified Caroline Bedford's asking. But it wasn't why I wanted to know.

"You'd better not rely on his repaying anything from what she's left him," Bates said.

"What do you mean?"

"She left him a hundred pounds."

"*What?*"

" 'To buy something to remember her by,' she put it."

I was astounded. "Who gets it, then?"

Again Bates hesitated, and I could almost feel his reluctance. "A man named Peter Stephen Hillyer gets most of it. But, for God's sake, keep that to yourself."

"Are you kidding?"

"No, of course not."

I had known he wasn't—some instinct had told me—and anyway, he wouldn't have joked about a thing like that. Not Bates.

"The Hillyer who lives at Hensbourn Green?" I asked him.

"Yes. Why? Do you know him?"

"He's the local public-school layabout. Drinks too much and owes money all over the place. Or so they say."

"Mrs. Sapsed described him as her 'dear friend.' "

Oh, no! I thought. She couldn't have been naïve enough to think people would take the words at their face value. Especially when she had left him almost everything and her husband next to nothing. It didn't need much imagination to guess what the press would make of that.

I wondered if Sapsed had known the terms of the will this morning; he had looked almost indifferent when Wheatley took the envelope from the deed-box and handed it to Bates. He was a comparatively poor man; he must have taken it for granted she had left him the bulk of her estate. But I knew now why Colin had looked so startled when he glanced through the will before he put it away in his brief-case.

"How much did she leave?" I asked. "Have you any idea?"

"Give us a chance. But it must add up to a good half million. The house was hers and that's worth at least a hundred thousand."

That was another shock. Why, if she was such a wealthy woman and the house had been hers, had Sapsed borrowed so heavily from the Bank for the work they had had done on it? I could see no logical reason, but logic had little to do with arrangements between husbands and wives. At least I knew now why Sapsed hadn't given the Bank a charge over the house to secure his borrowings.

"It's going to be a nasty shock for him if he doesn't know," I observed. "Who's going to tell him?"

"Can't you guess?" Bates said. "Me." He didn't sound exactly overjoyed at the prospect and I didn't blame him. "I'm seeing him at half-past three."

"At the house?"

"Yes."

"Can I come with you?"

I could imagine him frowning, weighing the pros and cons. There weren't many pros.

"Why?"

"I have to see him about one or two things and it'll save bothering him twice," I said, relying on his knowing little about inspection procedures.

"All right, I suppose so," he agreed ungraciously. "I'll pick you up at the branch at twenty past. Okay?"

"Thanks," I said. " 'Bye."

As I replaced the phone, I heard a slight movement behind

me and turned. Caroline Bedford had come into the room. I wondered how long she had been there and how much she had heard; I had been lying to Bates; there was no reason for my wanting to see Sapsed I could have justified if I had been challenged about it.

"Are you going to be using this room for long?" Miss Bedford enquired coolly.

"As long as it isn't inconvenient," I answered.

"I'm afraid it is. We have some customers who use it every Thursday afternoon to make up their wages; they're waiting outside now."

"Then, I'll go somewhere else," I said. She started walking out of the room. "Are you feeling better now?"

For a moment she stared at me. There was nothing friendly about her expression. "I told you, it was the room, it was too hot."

"Yes, of course. I'm sorry. What do you think it was shocked Sapsed so much when Wheatley opened the box?"

"Shocked him? Did anything?"

It seemed to me there was a challenge in the way she faced me. Probably it was unconscious. Or perhaps I imagined it; something about Caroline Bedford always made me feel I was being forced on to the defensive.

"Did you hear him say, 'Oh, God!'?" I asked her.

"If I did, I don't remember." She paused. "He must be under a terrible strain."

"Yes," I agreed, "he's having a bad time."

And this afternoon, when Bates told him about the will, he would have a worse time. It wasn't only the money, which he might or might not need—I suspected he did, badly—he would have to accept his wife had left almost everything to another man. To her "dear friend." She had preferred somebody who was widely despised to him. I wondered if Sapsed and Hillyer knew each other.

"Galleys will be able to use this room in five minutes, then?" Miss Bedford asked.

"They can use it now." I picked up my brief-case and followed her out. Through the glass panel in the security door I could see two men and a woman waiting on the other side of it in the banking-hall. For some reason, the sight of them reassured me. As if, subconsciously, I had suspected Caroline Bedford of inventing them and was glad to find she hadn't.

But why should she?

Going through to the annexe where the account cards were stored in two filing-cabinets, I searched among the H's until I found a card in the name of Peter Stephen Hillyer of Blackwells, Hensbourn Green. It told me nothing about him I didn't know, except that he was a customer.

Replacing the card, I went upstairs to the machine-room and looked at the last few months' ledger sheets for his account. It was overdrawn £16,730 and he had a loan with nearly £24,000 still outstanding. Hillyer's had been one of the accounts I had discussed with Waites, and I wondered why the name hadn't meant anything to me. It wasn't one of Waites' advances; he had inherited it from his more open-minded—or open-handed—predecessor. It looked like being a difficult debt to recover, £40,000 was the hell of a lot for a tenant farming 150 acres to be borrowing.

I glanced at the entries on the account. Apparently Hillyer hardly ever drew out any cash, and I wondered how he paid his wages—presumably he employed at least one man.

SEVEN

Bates arrived five minutes late complaining about the traffic. I suspected he was one of those people who are always late without meaning to be and that the prospect of keeping the Minister waiting was worrying him; E & T people spent a lot of their lives worrying. Perhaps it had something to do with the nature of their work.

"It'll only take a few minutes to get there," I told him.

He didn't look reassured and I supposed he was still dreading breaking the news of the will's terms to Sapsed. I didn't blame him; I wouldn't have looked forward to it myself.

"Who engrossed the will?" I asked as we drove up the Ridings in his car.

"A firm in Cambridge."

"Not Wheatley?"

"No. He did her last one, after she and Sapsed were married—he and Sapsed were the executors. He didn't know she was thinking about changing it. And the first we heard was when the Cambridge people wrote and told us she'd made a new will appointing us."

"When was that?"

"Three weeks ago. That's why nobody had got round to chasing the branch for it; you know we like to have a look at any will where we're the executor in case there's something in it may cause problems later."

"It's a pity you didn't see this one," I commented.

At least then they would have been forewarned. But perhaps ignorance was bliss; there would have been nothing they could do short of renouncing the appointment. I thought I knew why the dead woman had gone to solicitors in Cambridge; she didn't want Wheatley to know what she was doing. And that suggested she hadn't told her husband, either.

"You said, 'her last one,' " I pointed out. "How many wills did she make?"

"Wheatley says four. You know she'd been married twice before, don't you?"

I didn't and it came as a slight shock, though why it should I couldn't have said. "Who were the other husbands?" I asked. "Anyone well known?"

"I've no idea."

The house was a mile out of Lemsfield, beyond the Old Town. A drive led between paddocks which, near the house, were transformed into smooth lawns shaded by a magnificent cedar of Lebanon. I recognized it at once as the house I had seen on television on Monday evening, an attractive rectangular building with whitewashed walls and a tiled roof. It stood on fairly high ground, but the view of the river and the hills on the other side of the valley was obscured by the wood less than a quarter of a mile from the house. Somehow I had expected it to be farther away, and it occurred to me that, with the windows open as they must have been that hot night, it was surprising nobody in the house had heard Mrs. Sapsed cry out. Perhaps she hadn't had time. And her husband had left for London some time before, so that the only person in the house was the French *au pair*. The dogs were off their leads; if they had wandered away following scents through the wood, it would explain why they hadn't barked and attacked the murderer.

The house was large by modern standards, without being grand or pretentious. It looked as if it had been built as the home of a prosperous farmer. Bates pulled up in the gravelled space before the front door and we climbed out.

His ring was answered by a plain, stocky girl of about twenty with a sallow complexion and brown hair pulled back in a pony-tail. Beyond her I could see a tall, burly man in the shadows at the rear of the hall.

"We have an appointment to see Mr. Sapsed," Bates told her. "My name is Bates."

"Oh yes." The girl had a marked French accent.

Smiling uncertainly, she led us into a room at the front of the house and disappeared, saying she would tell Mr. Sapsed we were there. The room could have been photographed just as it was to illustrate an article in some glossy magazine: "The delightful Hertfordshire home of Mr. and Mrs. Gerald Sapsed." The carpet, I thought, was probably Persian, and there were some nice old landscapes on the walls. The furniture glowed in the sunlight.

Then Sapsed came in. He looked pale, but he was probably a man who never had much colour. When I shook hands with him, I could see the signs of strain round his eyes, but he looked composed. If he was surprised to find me there with Bates, he showed no sign of it; his manner was polite but reserved. It implied that this was another formality to be endured and he would be glad when we had gone; in the meantime he would treat us courteously.

For a minute or two we exchanged conventional pleasantries; then Bates asked, "May I ask whether you know the terms of Mrs. Sapsed's will, Mr. Sapsed?"

Was there a moment's hesitation before Sapsed replied, "No, I don't"?

"You knew she made a new will about a month ago?"

This time the pause was noticeable. "No," Sapsed said again.

Bates opened his brief-case, took out the envelope with its

Gothic lettering and, pressing the long edges until it was almost a cylinder, extracted the will. I felt myself growing tenser, but the Minister's face was devoid of expression.

Briefly Bates explained the terms. He had a rather high-pitched, nasal voice which now I found almost unbearable. Sapsed had his emotions under tight control, but I saw that the fingers of his right hand continually massaged the arm of his chair.

Bates' voice creaked on. I was watching Sapsed closely and I was pretty sure he had been telling the truth and he hadn't known the will's contents before. When Bates stopped, there was a tight little pause; then he said, "Thank you." That was all.

Bates and I sat there, and I wondered if he felt as uncomfortable as I did.

"Mr. Sapsed," I said, "I'm sorry to have to ask you this, but have you any idea what the money in those envelopes represented?"

He turned his head slightly to look at me, and I saw that his eyes were strangely blank, as if he were looking inwards at himself. "I've no idea," he answered. "Does it matter?"

"Probably not," I agreed. "There were some dates on the envelopes."

He made no comment and Bates began talking about the formalities of the inquest and funeral. I excused myself and walked out to the hall. There was no sign of the French girl or the tall man, but from the back of the house I could hear the clatter of pans. I opened the door across the hall and looked inside. Then, closing it again, I did the same with the other two doors.

Sapsed and Bates would be several minutes yet. I let myself out by the front door. Two golden labradors were lying in the sun. They lifted their magnificent heads when I appeared, and one of them got to its feet with almost arthritic slowness and lolloped over. It was too well bred to actually sniff at my trouser-legs, but it looked up and wagged its tail slowly. Its companion ambled over to join us. I supposed they were the dogs Rosemary Sapsed had taken for a walk last night. If so, and they were pining for her, they were even better at concealing their grief than their master.

I patted their heads and walked round the side of the house, away from the room where Sapsed and Bates were sitting. I had nearly reached the back and was on the point of turning round when the French girl came out. Seeing me, she stopped, startled. Then she recognized me.

"Mr. Sapsed and Mr. Bates are still talking," I said.

She nodded.

"You must be Mademoiselle Chabrier."

"Yes, *monsieur.*"

"All this must be horrible for you."

"*Oui,* eet ees." She eyed me warily. "You are from the police, no?"

"No," I told her, "the bank."

"*Ah, oui, la banque.*" She seemed reassured.

"Whereabouts in France do you come from?" I asked her.

"Angers. You know eet?"

"Not really; I've driven through it. Have you been here long?"

"Eight months."

"Your English is very good."

It was true, and she smiled, pleased by the compliment. "Thank you, *monsieur.*"

"Everybody seems to have liked Mrs. Sapsed," I remarked.

To my surprise the girl seemed suddenly to withdraw into herself. "Yes, *monsieur,*" she agreed without conviction. The relationship between the mistress of a house and an *au pair* wasn't always easy, or so I had read, and I wondered if there had been friction between this girl and the dead woman.

"You like it here?" I asked.

"Oh yes." No reservations there, at least.

"I must go back," I said. "Mr. Bates will be waiting for me."

But instead of retracing my steps I walked on round the back of the house, where there was a terrace overlooking more lawns and rose-beds, and along the other side. It was very quiet. I saw nobody, and even the dogs had gone to sleep again.

I was leaning against Bates' car, thinking about the house and what I had seen—or not seen—when he came out with Sapsed. They shook hands; then the Minister went back into the house and Bates walked over to where I was waiting.

"Where did you get to?" he demanded petulantly. Anything unpredictable made him uneasy.

"I thought you'd rather discuss the funeral without me there," I told him.

"You wanted to come."

"I know. Thanks very much." I had no intention of telling him my reasons for asking him to bring me; he would disapprove and he might tell somebody else.

I got into the car, and after a second or two of disapproving silence he did the same.

"Did you get the impression Sapsed knew what was in the will already?" I asked as he turned out of the drive.

"No." Bates sounded surprised. "He said he didn't. You heard him."

"Yes," I agreed. I thought I had noticed the hesitation before he said it too. All the same, I believed Bates was right. "Did he say anything about Hillyer after I left?"

"No."

It was obvious Bates didn't like my questions, so I let it go at that and we drove the rest of the way back into the town in silence. To save him driving all the way round, I got out in the

Ridings and walked the rest of the way. Today, I reminded myself, was Friday; this evening Laura would be home.

Millie Gant was walking towards the manager's room as I came through the security door. "There's a call for you," she told me. "Cathy's been trying to find you."

"I've been out with Colin Bates," I said. "Thanks, Millie."

I went into the waiting-room, picked up the receiver and told Cathy Pallett, the telephonist, that I was back.

It was Laura on the line, and as soon as she spoke I knew something was amiss.

"David? Darling, I'm sorry, I shan't be able to come home this weekend."

It was like her to come straight to the point, even though I could hear her distress.

"What's happened?" I asked, my spirits sinking.

"Mother's not very well." She hesitated, hating having to put it into words, as if that would make fear become reality. "The doctors are worried; it's worse than they thought."

"Oh." What else could I say? That I was sorry? I didn't have to tell her that; we were too close.

"I can't come and leave Dad on his own just now."

"No, of course not. Do you want me to come up?"

"Oh, darling, I wasn't going to ask you. Could you?"

"Of course I can." I tried to work out how long it would take me to drive home, collect a few things, then on to the dreary Midlands town to which Laura's parents had moved from Cressford. "I'll be there about half-past eight."

"Oh, David, thank you. I'll feel better if you're here."

What was so wonderful about driving a hundred miles on a fine spring evening to be with your wife when her mother was gravely ill? What was she thanking me for? Because she was frightened, I thought. She was scared her mother was going to die, and death was something she had never had to face at first-hand.

"Try not to worry," I told her.

"I will. Goodbye, darling."

She shouldn't sound so relieved—there would be nothing I could do—but I was glad she did . . . and ashamed of my disappointment that we wouldn't be spending the weekend together at home. The trouble was Laura's mother and I had never got on well. She hadn't liked her only child sleeping with a married man, even if his wife had walked out on him before they met and they were getting married as soon as they could. I didn't blame her for that, and I suppose, deep down, she was afraid it would happen again and this time it would be Laura who suffered. But she didn't have to show her disapproval in such spiteful ways now we were married and she could see Laura was happy.

Her attitude embarrassed Mr. Stearn. For him almost anything Laura did was all right and we had always got on well. But I knew how deeply he cared for his wife and what he must be suffering now.

I had paid my bill at the Lamb and cleared my room before I left this morning; now I had to ring and ask if I could have the room next week after all. I was lucky: nobody had booked it.

Just before five I left the bank, bought a *Standard* and a local paper from the old man on the corner and made my way to the car-park. Inevitably the murder made the main story on the front pages of both papers, but there was nothing in the reports I didn't already know. I tossed them on to the seat beside me, started the engine and drove out into the rush-hour traffic.

It was later than I had hoped before I got away from home. For one thing, I went round to tell Diane Foster, next door, that we wouldn't be home for the weekend, and she kept me talking for several minutes. Diane and Nigel, her husband, were good friends as well as neighbours, and she wanted to ask after Laura's mother.

Reckoning there would be the usual heavy Friday evening traffic on the southern stretches of the M1, I cut across by lesser roads and joined the motorway at Milton Keynes. From there I made good time to the interchange north of Rugby and along the M6 until I reached the outskirts of Birmingham. Nevertheless it was nearly nine o'clock before I pulled up outside the modest detached house Laura's parents had bought when they moved from Cressford.

Her father wasn't a man who showed his feelings much, but I thought he was glad to see me. The last time we met he had looked younger than his age, more like fifty-four than sixty-four. Now he seemed to have shrunk, the humorous light had gone from his eyes and the strain of the last few weeks was beginning to show in his face. He didn't try to hide his anxiety, and paradoxically that made it easier to talk to him.

The next afternoon, he and I went to see Mrs. Stearn in the hospital while Laura did some work about the house. There was no obvious change in her mother's appearance since I had last seen her, three months before, and I felt awkward talking to her. Probably it would have made little difference if our relationship had been easier. She talked brightly, but it was mostly to her husband, excluding me so that I felt I was an intruder and not really wanted there.

In the evening I stayed behind while Laura went with her father. With nothing worth watching on television and little else to do, I started thinking about the murder. I still found it hard to believe it was the work of a political fanatic. Would a man—or a woman—like that have waited in the wood, perhaps for hours, on the off-chance that Rosemary Sapsed would come that way? Throwing a brick, even a bomb, through a window would have made sense of a sort, but not that patient vigil, then stabbing her three times and walking away, taking the knife. To me they seemed to be the actions of somebody driven by a more personal hatred. Moreover, the dead woman appeared to have been genuinely liked by almost everybody who knew her. They accepted that her remarks on television were out of character, spoken in the stress of the moment. Only a madman, surely, could have resented them to the point of killing her?

But if the killer wasn't a madman, who was he? Hillyer had a motive if he knew the terms of the will, and, ironically, Sapsed if he didn't. What was the truth about the farmer's relationship with Mrs. Sapsed? Had she been his mistress? The wording of her will was either naïve in the extreme or coolly calculated—and I didn't see her as naïve. It seemed almost as if she had set out deliberately to wound her husband.

Another thought occurred to me: If she and Hillyer had been lovers and they had fallen out, that would provide him with another motive. Not only might he have hated her, he might have been afraid she would change her will again. And according to the talk in the Lamb, he was a man with a violent temper. True, he didn't strike me as likely to lie in wait for his victim with a knife; it would have been more in character for him to strangle her with his bare hands or blast half her head away with a shot-gun, but no-one could forecast how a man would react if he was put under enough pressure. It seemed unlikely they had arranged to meet in the wood—they were hardly star-crossed young lovers—but Hillyer needed money desperately and that had led plenty of better men than him to act out of character.

If Sapsed had known about the affair, it strengthened his motive too.

I told myself it was no concern of mine. The Sapseds might be—or, in Mrs. Sapsed's case, have been—customers of the

Bank, but her death was a matter for the police. This time I must leave well enough alone; the Chief had warned me.

The feeling that I was an outsider and contributing nothing persisted. On Sunday morning, Laura was too busy cooking lunch to want me around, and in the afternoon she went to the hospital with her father. The doctors had taken more X-rays and carried out more tests, but the results wouldn't be known for two or three days.

They got home just after five, and I dragged Laura out again for a walk. There was a park not far from the house, and we strolled aimlessly between the families with young children, the courting couples and the old people, the shadow of her mother's illness like a barrier between us. I wondered if she knew I wanted to be as involved, as worried as she was and couldn't because there was too much bitterness, too much misunderstanding between her mother and me.

Perhaps it was inevitable that in the end we should argue. And that because we each saw the other's side but were not prepared to admit it, the trivial difference became a quarrel. We walked back to the house, and as soon as I decently could I left and drove home.

EIGHT

Home was a three-bedroomed semi on a newish estate on the south side of Cressford between the London Road and the motorway. When Laura and I paid the deposit, just before we were married, it was two feet of brickwork, a square of concrete and not much else except a lot of dirt; it had been the autumn before it was completed and we could move in. Most of the people who lived on the estate were young or youngish, either still childless or with young children, and at night it was very quiet.

I had stopped at a service area on the motorway for a meal and it was nearly ten before I turned off the main road through the lanes that constituted the short cut home. Here between the hedges it was almost dark and the Triumph's headlights shone on the dense new foliage. The elms had gone, victims of Dutch elm disease, but plenty of oaks and sycamores and beeches remained.

I turned right opposite the Three Ducks, then right again into our road. Save for a Ford Capri parked against the kerb on the other side some way along, it was deserted. Dim squares of light showed where families were at home, reading or watching television. The Capri was parked without lights, and as I drove down the hill for a moment, the Triumph's lights illuminated it and I saw a man in the driving-seat. I wondered who it was sitting out there in a darkened car. Then I swung left on to our drive and both he and the car slid sideways, out of my range of vision. By the time I had locked the garage and found my front-door key, I had almost forgotten them.

I switched on the hall light, closed the front door behind me and was reaching out to open the door of the lounge when I heard a noise like that of another door closing quite near. I stopped, my fingers on the handle; it had seemed to come from the rear of the house. For three or four seconds I stood there, tense, my ears straining for any other sound, but there was nothing. It was only a few feet to the kitchen door; I spent another five seconds listening to silence, then thrust it open hard.

Nothing happened. Outside, in the road, a car started up and drove past, accelerating fast. I pressed the light-switch. The fluorescent tube flickered two or three times, then came on, flooding the kitchen with its harsh brilliance. I blinked and stopped dead.

A man was lying on the floor between me and the cooker. He was on his face, bent arms reaching out each side of his head, his left leg doubled up. It was Nigel Foster, our next-door neighbour.

Oh, God! I thought. I bent over him. At least he was breathing fairly normally.

There was a movement behind me and I turned quickly. Diane was in the doorway staring at us.

"Nigel!" she gasped. "David, what—Oh no!"

I saw the horror in her eyes harden into suspicion. "I've just come in," I told her. "I didn't hit him, I found him like this. What was he doing here?"

"We thought we saw a light—like somebody with a torch. Nigel came round to have a look." Diane squatted on her heels beside him. "He's all right, isn't he?"

How could I tell? "He seems okay," I said. "I'll call the doctor. Who do you go to?"

"Doctor Graham. I don't know his number."

I went out to the phone in the hall and looked in the directory for Dr. Graham's home number. He answered the phone himself and promised he would come straight round. I pressed down the rest and dialled the police; they said they would come round too.

By the time I returned to the kitchen, Nigel was sitting up and taking notice. He explained that when he and Diane came home from visiting her mother and thought they saw somebody with a torch moving about in the house, he had used Laura's key she had left with them in case of an emergency to get in by the front door. In the hall he had stopped without switching on the light and listened. He thought he heard a sound in the kitchen, but when he opened the door it was nearly dark and as he stepped forward, something struck him hard on his head and he passed out.

A minute or two later, Diane had heard me come home and decided to join us, partly to see if Nigel had found anything and partly to ask after Laura's mother. She had seen the light in the kitchen, come round to the back door and found it unlocked.

"I didn't unlock it," I said.

"Neither did I," Nigel added.

Whoever it was knocked out Nigel must have heard me come in at the front door and escaped by the back. I remembered the car I had heard as I came into the kitchen.

"Did you hear a car driving off just after I came in?" I asked Diane.

She thought for a moment. "Yes. Yes, I did. It was parked outside the Fergusons'; I saw it as I came round. Why?"

"You didn't see a man run out and get into it?"

"No, it was pretty dark and I wasn't taking much notice. It hadn't been there long; I saw it pull up when I went out to fetch the kids' toys." She stopped. "You think it belonged to whoever coshed Nigel?"

"It could." A dark Capri, I thought. There must be thousands of them about. Hundreds of thousands, probably.

"Hadn't you better see if he took anything?" Diane asked.

It was funny, I hadn't thought of that; I had been too concerned with seeing Nigel was all right and finding out why he was here. Now I made a quick tour of the house. There was no time for a thorough check, but as far as I could see nothing was missing. None of the obvious, more valuable things anyway.

I had just finished and rejoined the others in the lounge when the doctor arrived. He gave Nigel a brief examination and said he didn't think any serious damage had been done but Nigel had better go to the hospital for a proper check.

As he was leaving, the police came, two uniformed constables, one middle-aged, the other about twenty-two. They listened politely while I explained as concisely as I could what had happened; then the younger one went out of the room. I heard him go to the front door, then down the hall to the kitchen. His colleague walked over to the window, gave it a cursory glance and sat down on the settee, knees wide apart, holding his cap.

"Is there anything missing?" he asked me.

"Not as far as I can see," I replied.

For all the response I got I might have been speaking to a brick wall. We sat in silence until, after two or three minutes, the younger one returned.

"There's no sign of forcible entry," he reported.

"Not here either." The middle-aged one stood up. "We'll make inquiries."

He seemed to have lost any slight interest he might have had in the intruder; nobody had broken in and nothing had been stolen. Perhaps he suspected Nigel had imagined the light and knocked himself out falling and hitting his head on the kitchen table.

"Look," Diane said. She was a friendly, good-natured woman as a rule, but she had a low boiling-point and she was close to it now. "Whoever it was in here attacked my husband. What are you going to do about it?"

The older policeman regarded her impassively. "We'll make inquiries," he said. Somehow the words carried no more conviction now he had repeated them. Perhaps he realized it and that was why he added, "Somebody will probably be round tomorrow to take a statement."

"Oh, thank you very much," Diane said bitterly.

I thought the younger policeman was looking uncomfortable. "You've no idea who it could have been?" he asked. We shook our heads. "You didn't see him and you think he may have driven away in a dark Capri." He didn't shrug, but he might as well have done.

"My God!" Diane exclaimed.

I had seen enough of the police in the course of my work to have a healthy respect for them generally, but these two weren't doing anything to enhance it. They believed the task of finding whoever had forced his way into the house and coshed Nigel was hopeless and they didn't want to know.

There didn't seem much we could do about it. Not then, at least. They asked one or two more questions—strictly for appearances, I thought—and departed. I told myself perhaps we were imagining their indifference and their seeming lack of interest was a screen, but I didn't believe it.

The next morning, Rosemary Sapsed's murder had been relegated to an inside page in the *Telegraph;* the lead-story was the continuing crisis in NATO. The editorial contained a discreetly worded comment that it was doubly unfortunate that at this time the Minister of Defence should have suffered a personal tragedy. In other words, he couldn't give all his attention to NATO's affairs.

There was no bread in the house, but I found some crisp-bread in the kitchen cupboard and ate two of them with butter and marmalade, washing them down with orange juice. When I had finished, I fetched my brief-case and was about to put my paper in it when I noticed the wad of envelopes at the bottom. Once again I nearly threw them away, but something, an instinct, curiosity perhaps, stopped me. I put the paper on top of them and closed the case.

Diane was in the kitchen next door. She reported that apart from a headache and a lump on his head Nigel was all right. She was still furious with the two policemen for their lack of interest, and it was several minutes before I could get away. When I did, I started the Triumph thoughtfully and backed out into the road. Why had they displayed so little concern? True, nothing had been stolen, but Nigel had been laid out and I would have expected them to welcome a break in the monotony. They hadn't been good actors, and now, looking back, it seemed almost as if they had been working to orders. But why? On impulse, at the end of the road I turned right towards the town, parked in the square and walked round to the police station. It wasn't the first time I had been inside the gaunt old building and I wondered a trifle uneasily if anyone there would recognize me and remember the other occasions. Then it had been only John Parker's powers of persuasion and my own good fortune that had saved me from something a good deal worse than the telling-off I had received from Superintendent Harper.

This time I saw the duty sergeant, a large, square-faced man of about forty-five with close-cropped, sandy hair. He listened politely, his expression giving nothing away, while I told him what had happened last night.

"Yes?" he said when I had finished. It could equally well have been a statement or a question.

"I wondered if there was any news," I explained.

"I'm afraid I can't tell you."

"What does that mean?"

He straightened up as if the interview was over. "I believe inquiries are proceeding."

Inquiries will be made. Are being made. Are proceeding. Helping the police with their inquiries. It was jargon. They were euphemisms to conceal—what? In this case, was it that the police were doing nothing? Intended to do nothing? I felt a sudden surge of anger.

"That's all?" I demanded.

"All?" The sergeant regarded me stonily.

"Oh, thank you," I said bitterly.

I walked out into the street and back to the square. I was convinced the sergeant had known more than he was prepared—or allowed—to tell me. Almost, it was as if the police knew who had been in the house last night and were protecting him. The idea that in England one's home was inviolate was so deeply entrenched it was hard to believe they could be involved. What was going on? Who had decided it didn't matter that Nigel had been attacked and left unconscious? That it had happened was disturbing enough; the suspicion that the police might be covering up for the culprit disturbed me a whole lot more.

I drove to Lemsfield without being more than half aware of what I was doing. Nearly there I only just escaped crashing into a lorry which had the right of way at a road junction— and the fact that I did owed nothing to me.

Ben and Trevor had just arrived when I reached the bank. I left them and the rest of the team to carry on with the routine of the inspection, collected what I needed and took myself off to the waiting-room.

I had been there about twenty minutes when Millie Gant tapped on the door, put her head round it and said, "Caroline's looking for some envelopes. She says they were in Mrs.

Sapsed's deed-box and she thought you might know what happened to them."

I wondered why Miss Bedford should be interested in fourteen grubby envelopes which had been discarded days ago. An idea, surely too fantastic to be true, occurred to me; what connection could there possibly be between the envelopes and the man who had been in my house last night? It was simply that both related to something unexplained which had aroused my curiosity. All the same, I decided I would have another look at the envelopes before I parted with them.

"Why does she want them?" I asked Millie.

"I don't know."

"Tell her I'm sorry but I can't help, will you?" It wasn't altogether a lie; I couldn't help. Or wouldn't.

Millie began to withdraw her head.

"Do you happen to know if Mr. Sapsed's rung this morning?" I enquired as casually as I could. It was a wild guess, no more.

"Yes, Caroline spoke to him about ten minutes ago," Millie replied. "Did you want him?"

"No," I said, "it doesn't matter."

She went out, closing the door behind her, and I tried to get on with the work I had been doing before she came. But I couldn't concentrate. There was a feeling I couldn't escape that I was becoming involved in something I didn't understand, and I didn't like it.

Just after ten-thirty I went up to the staff-room for coffee. I was gone about fifteen minutes, and when I came down again I found Caroline Bedford in the waiting-room, standing by the desk. My brief-case was on the floor beside her and, although I had no real reason for suspecting her of trying to open it, nevertheless I was glad I always locked it when I was leaving it unattended.

"I came to get some booklets," she explained with rather

more defiance in her tone than seemed necessary. She had two or three of the Bank's leaflets clutched in her left hand.

"That's all right," I said.

She went out, leaving me thinking that most people automatically used their stronger hands to pick up things and I had never noticed she was left-handed. Had she suspected I was lying when I told Millie I couldn't help over the envelopes, waited until I was out of the room and then, armed with an excuse for being there if I returned, come and tried to look in my case? It seemed pretty unlikely, but so did a lot of other things that had happened lately.

I wondered if it was coincidence that within a few minutes of her receiving a phone call from Gerald Sapsed she had asked Millie to find out if I knew what had happened to the envelopes. Somehow I didn't think so; she had shown no interest in them before. But what reason could Sapsed have given her for wanting them and why had she gone to such lengths to try to recover them for him?

Unlocking my brief-case, I extracted the thin wad in its rubber band. Ordinary, rather soiled envelopes with nothing interesting or remarkable about them that I could see. Why had Sapsed wanted them? For that matter, why had I bothered to save them and then lied about still having them? They weren't mine.

They weren't Sapsed's, either; they had been in his wife's deed-box and she had left him precisely one hundred pounds. Nothing more. If anybody, I supposed they belonged to our E & T people until probate was granted, when, presumably, they would pass to Hillyer.

I put them back in my case and locked it.

NINE

Caroline Bedford took her lunch-hour from twelve to one. I told Ben and the others I wouldn't be joining them today, waited until I saw her walk past the open door of the waiting-room and followed her. She turned left along the crescent, then left again into the Ridings. It was easy to keep her in sight; she walked well, with a confident, almost arrogant stride, and today she was wearing a cream jacket with a pale green skirt. Once or twice she paused to look in a shop window, but I was a good fifty yards behind her and I was fairly sure she hadn't spotted me. Once, three girls walking towards me hid her for several seconds, and when they had passed I could no longer see her. For a moment I thought she must have gone into one of the shops and I swore under my breath; even if I knew which one I could hardly follow her in, and she might be twenty minutes trying on shoes or dresses.

Then I noticed that just beyond where I had last seen her there was a small restaurant. It was the sort of place I would have expected her to favour, the kind that serves salads and home-made food, but it wasn't my taste and I felt a pang of regret for the pint and sandwiches I might have enjoyed in a pub with the rest of the team. Pushing the door open, I walked in.

Inside, the restaurant was larger and more attractive than it had appeared from the street. The furniture and decor were modern and the pictures on the walls pleasant if not very distinguished originals by local artists. There was little visible plastic and no mock-Tudor beams. Miss Bedford was sitting by herself at a table for two in a sort of alcove, studying the menu. Either it was surprisingly engrossing or she had other things on her mind; I was standing beside her before she noticed me.

I would have had to be pretty conceited to think she was pleased. She frowned. But her tone wasn't actually hostile when she said, "Hallo."

"May I join you?" I sat down facing her without giving her time to answer. "Do you come here often?"

"Sometimes. When I want to be alone." She put down the menu and unbuttoned her jacket. Then, as if to make amends, she added, "The food's quite good."

Quite good, I thought. The middle-class woman's need of qualification, the fear of showing enthusiasm for anything. A fear of commitment. Was Caroline Bedford afraid of committing herself?

As I reached out for the menu, she drew her hand away as if she were afraid mine might touch it and picked up a knife. It was a conscious gesture, and I knew I was meant to see it.

The waitress came, and Miss Bedford ordered the quiche and salad. It seemed a safe choice and I did the same.

"Did you know Mrs. Sapsed?" I asked when the girl had gone.

"Only to say good morning to. Why?" Although she had answered calmly enough I had seen her tense, and the fingers holding the knife had tightened.

"I just wondered. Everybody seems to have liked her; she'll be missed here, won't she?"

"Yes."

"They say she did a lot to help her husband."

"So I believe."

"It must be a deadly existence being a politician's wife, having to listen to him spouting the same old rubbish, the same old clichés week after week and pretending to think they're fresh and wonderful. And always smiling. Most politicians are ham actors. Or shysters." I was trying to anger her, to get under her skin, because I suspected she knew Sapsed—and, possibly, had known his wife—better than she was ready to say. She had to for him to ring her and ask her to get back the envelopes. And perhaps there was another reason, one I was hardly prepared to admit even to myself: that I found her attractive and her aloofness taunted me. But she just sat there and took it, her only visible reaction an almost indiscernible tightening of the muscles of her face. She was hating me.

"Look at Sapsed," I went on, despising myself for what I was doing. "I don't suppose he knows how to be sincere about anything."

There was a moment's silence; then she asked coolly, contemptuously, "Why are you so interested in them? Do you get some sort of kick out of other people's tragedies? I can imagine you slowing down to look when you're driving past an accident."

Her contempt got to me and I felt myself flushing. "I like to know what people are really like," I said. "What makes them tick."

For the first time since I joined her, she smiled. It wasn't a friendly smile. "*You* talk about clichés," she observed witheringly.

I grinned. "Touché. Did you find those envelopes?"

"No."

If I had hoped to catch her off guard I had failed. "Why did you want them?"

"I didn't particularly. I just thought perhaps we should keep them in case the police or E & T wanted them."

It was possible. "Why should they?" I asked.

"I've no idea."

"I thought it was Sapsed who wanted them."

The slender, fastidious curves of her eyebrows rose. "Why should he?"

"It must have been something somebody said. He phoned you about them, didn't he?"

"No. If you really want to know, he rang about his overdraft. That should please you."

The waitress returned with our quiches and salads, and for the next minute or two we busied ourselves with condiments and dressings.

"He'll be a wealthy man now, I suppose," I remarked, breaking the silence.

"I suppose so." Miss Bedford helped herself to cole slaw.

There was no reason why she should know the terms of Rosemary Sapsed's will, I reminded myself. Unless Bates and I were both wrong, Sapsed himself hadn't known them until Friday afternoon and it was unlikely he would rush to tell her. More likely the opposite, and he would postpone as long as he could her finding out that he could no longer count on any money from that source to repay his borrowing from the bank.

"Have you seen the work he had done to the house?" I asked.

"No."

"There wasn't any. I was out there on Friday with Colin Bates; there's no sign of anything having been done to the house for years."

For a moment the silence was almost tangible; then Caroline Bedford asked bitterly, "Is that all you're interested in? What all this is about?"

"All what?"

"You follow me here, sit down without waiting to see if I mind and do nothing but talk about the Sapseds. Are you so concerned about his bloody accounts?"

It was the first time I had heard her swear, and there was something almost endearing about it. You could tell she didn't swear often, she sounded like a little girl daring to use a word she knew she shouldn't in front of grown-ups.

"No," I said. "Let's talk about something else."

"I'd rather not talk to you at all." She took three pound notes from her handbag, slapped them down on the table and stood up. "Goodbye."

I watched her walk out. Very upright. Not fast enough to attract attention but more quickly than she would have done if I hadn't angered her. It was no good my telling myself I had done nothing to be ashamed of; there had been sufficient truth in her accusation to leave me feeling guilty. Just a little.

I supposed I should take the envelopes to the police. But there were no grounds for supposing they had anything to do with the murder, and I had been accused of interfering before. This time I would leave well enough alone.

I finished my salad, and when the waitress came, asked for apple pie and cream and explained that my companion had had to go back to her office. I had no intention of allowing Miss Bedford to spoil my lunch; what she did with hers was her own affair.

An important part of every inspection is the interviewing and reporting on the members of the branch staff. At Lemsfield, Ben was to see the junior people while I interviewed the senior half, and when I got back to the bank after lunch I found he had already taken over the staff-room and started. Trevor was with Gordon Hodgson, going through the list of securities queries he had left with him last week. I decided I might as well make a start on my own interviews and went in search of the second cashier, a girl named Margaret Storey.

By the time we finished for the day, I had seen six people, which left twice as many still to be seen. I considered asking Caroline Bedford if, in view of her obvious dislike of me, she would prefer Ben to write her report, but rejected the idea;

she would be shown what I had written before the report left
the branch and could object then if there was anything in it
she thought unwarranted. To hand over the job to Ben would
smack of shirking responsibility, and I wasn't going to display
that kind of weakness to her. In any case, by now she was
probably regretting her behaviour at lunch-time.

As we said goodbye to Harry Roche and left, I promised
myself that this evening I would go for a walk, have a quiet
drink and, if there was anything on worth seeing, watch some
television. A pleasant, relaxing evening. I wouldn't even think
about Rosemary Sapsed's murder.

And I would ring Laura. What was it they said about not
letting the sun go down on one's wrath? Well, it had gone
down once already on mine and the wrath had long since
evaporated. I wondered if Laura was waiting for me to ring,
hoping I would but reluctant, half-afraid of taking the initia-
tive herself.

There were only three or four other people staying at the
Lamb, and usually I was the first back in the evenings, so that
when I parked the TR7 in the yard, the only cars there were
the manager's Alfasud and a battered old 1100 which belonged to one of the staff. This evening there was a third, a
grey Ford Capri Ghia.

Vickie was behind the reception desk. I bought a local paper and decided that if I rang Laura now she would be back
from the hospital but not yet busy getting supper. There was
nobody in the phone-box by the stairs; I dialled her father's
number and waited, hoping she would answer.

She did, and I could tell from her voice she had wanted me
to call. We talked for several minutes and I felt a good deal
easier in my own mind. Perhaps my conscience had been
more troubled than I had thought. I replaced the phone and
went up to my room, glancing at the front page of the *Star*.

When I entered the dining-room, soon after seven, the new

arrival was already there, sitting by himself at a table with his back to one of the windows. Most of the Lamb's clientèle were reps and junior managers on courses at the local factories —he didn't look like either. He was about forty, tall and athletically built. His dark hair was cut fairly short and he possessed the sort of features women journalists called "rugged good looks." A solid citizen who voted Conservative, held down very efficiently some senior executive job and played golf to a single-figure handicap. His name was Roberts.

He was still there, lingering over his coffee, when I finished my meal and left the dining-room to go up to my room. Five minutes later, when I came downstairs again, he had gone. I went for my walk.

When I returned, the bar was nearly deserted and there was a lethargic air about it. Danny was taking his time wiping a glass, as if he was interested in seeing how long he could make it last. A man sitting by himself at the bar looked up as I walked in. It was Martyn Carthy, Sapsed's agent, and rather to my surprise he recognized me and called, "Hallo."

I joined him.

"What'll you have?" he asked.

I told him a bitter, and he asked Danny for a pint. We watched in silence as Danny drew it, two steady pulls on the handle, then another, shorter one. He held the glass steady while the head formed and overflowed gently down the sides, then handed it to me. Martyn paid him.

"Cheers," I said, sipping my beer. "How're things with you?"

He looked depressed. "Bloody awful."

"It's difficult?"

He gave me a quick sideways glance, then looked away again. "Why d'you say that?"

He had slurred the words, and I realized for the first time

that he wasn't sober. Not incapably drunk, either, but he had had enough already this evening to shed a good many of his inhibitions. It wouldn't take much more to destroy the rest.

"I thought the police would be asking a lot of questions. And there's the NATO business," I said.

"Police haven't bothered me. It's Gerald. Poor devil, Gerald. Has to keep coming back here."

"How's he taking it?"

Again Carthy gave me that quick, almost furtive look. "All right."

"He'll miss his wife. Helping here, I mean."

"You think so?" Carthy drank a good part of the whisky left in his glass.

I was startled by the disillusionment in his voice; it wasn't the cynicism of the drunk, either. I didn't want to stay there listening to him, but he had aroused my curiosity.

"You didn't like her?" I suggested.

"Like her?" Carthy laughed bitterly. "Rosemary was a bitch."

"You're not serious?" I said.

"Course I'm serious."

"I thought everybody liked her."

"Tha's right, ev'rybody liked Rosemary." The descent into maudlin drunkenness had come quite suddenly. "They didn't know what she was really like. Nobody knew 'cept Gerald an' me."

Somewhere at the back of my mind was the memory of something I had heard, something which had suggested not everybody liked the dead woman. What was it? I couldn't remember. Danny was eyeing us uneasily. Perhaps he expected me to do something about Carthy. But what could I do, short of carrying him home, wherever that was? I walked over to where Danny was interminably wiping another glass.

"Is he often like this?" I asked him quietly.

"I've never seen him like it before," he replied.

Thank you, too, I thought meanly. Why did it have to be me who got stuck with him on the one and only occasion? I would have liked to walk out; it was none of my business and I didn't want to become involved. But I couldn't just leave him there.

"What are we going to do with him?" I asked.

"I'd sooner he was out of here," Danny muttered.

The other customers were watching and listening. They must have heard what Carthy had been saying.

"Where does he live?" I asked.

"I'll find out."

"You do that and I'll drive him home," I said.

You bloody fool, I thought; you need your head examined, taking on responsibility for a self-pitying drunk I hardly knew and who would probably thank me by vomiting in my nice clean car. Sod him.

Danny was gone two or three minutes. I guessed he was looking for Carthy's address in the local Kelly's or the phone book.

"43, Conway Court," he told me when he returned. "It's a block of flats in Hill Street. You can't miss it, you turn off opposite the civic hall."

"I'll find it," I promised.

Danny grinned. "The best of British."

Sod you, too, I thought.

To my relief, Carthy made no objection to going with me. Indeed, he seemed only too glad to, though I had to half carry him out to the Triumph. Once in it, he slumped in the passenger seat and looked as if he was going to sleep. I got in beside him, started the engine and drove out of the yard.

We were half-way down the hill to the New Town when he said suddenly and quite clearly, "She hated Gerald. She was trying to destroy him. Did you see her on tel'vision th' other

THE GARB OF TRUTH

night? She did that on purpose—like she did th' other things."

Again the memory of something forgotten haunted me. "Why should she?" I asked him. I wasn't really interested; all I wanted was to get him home and off my hands, as intact as possible.

"Because she was all twisted up. She was a bitch. Did you know that?"

No, I thought, I hadn't known it, and I wondered if, just possibly, everybody else was wrong and it was true. There had been hints: I remembered the French girl's flat "Yes, *monsieur*," when I remarked that everybody seemed to have liked Mrs. Sapsed. And the next moment I remembered what it was that had been haunting me: the evening Waites introduced me to Carthy and the Hendersons, Mrs. Henderson had said something about things Rosemary Sapsed had done before the interview on television, implying they had probably hurt her husband. I felt vaguely uncomfortable, as if I were watching veils being stripped from the dead woman, revealing too much which should have remained concealed. Had Antony been right, and the evil men did, did live after them? Whatever she had done while she was alive, she had paid for it; let her rest in peace now. Anyway, Carthy was drunk; he was probably exaggerating.

There was another possibility: that he had loyally accepted what Sapsed had told him. He had lost his grip on lucidity again now and I guessed he had forgotten who I was—to him I was just a pair of ears to listen. Perhaps he didn't even care whether I listened any longer; he was talking for his own benefit, to spew out whatever it was festering inside him. I was disgusted, with him and with myself for being part of his degradation.

He wasn't much help locating his flat, but we made it eventually. It was on the third floor and the lift wasn't working.

Somehow, by cajoling him along and the use of a little brute force, I got him up the stairs and into an armchair. From some vague idea that it was the right thing to do, I loosened his tie and undid the top button of his shirt. At least he hadn't been sick on the way.

Having deposited him safely, I looked round. It was a commonplace room, the home of a bachelor who spent little time there and who, when he did, didn't care much about his surroundings. I should know, I had lived in one very like it once. There was a record player on a table by one wall, a pile of records beside it, two or three books scattered about and more on a shelf. I was more interested in a framed photograph on the sideboard, a studio portrait of a woman. The woman was Rosemary Sapsed. Across the bottom she had scrawled, "With love to Martyn—Rosemary". A conventional inscription or something else? Whatever there might have been between them once, friendship or something deeper, it had been over before she died. But how long before?

Carthy was asleep. I let myself out and drove back to the Lamb, parked the TR7 in the yard and was locking the door when I saw my brief-case. It must have slid off the passenger seat at some time, probably when I had to brake hard on the way from the bank this afternoon, and I had overlooked it when I got out. Picking it up, I went into the hotel. The prospect of another drink didn't appeal to me, but I glanced into the bar as I passed on my way to my room. The new arrival, Roberts, was sitting at a table by himself, reading a magazine.

I met no-one on the stairs, and the first-floor landing was deserted. I pushed my key into the lock, turned it and pushed. The door opened.

I don't know what told me somebody had been in the room. It was nothing tangible, no more than a feeling, the sort of thing which makes the hair rise on a dog's back, but I was sure. I walked over to the dressing-table. When I went to it after getting back from the bank this afternoon a corner of a shirt-tail had caught in the frame of the bottom drawer as I shut it. I had noticed the tiny piece of fabric hanging out but couldn't be bothered to do anything about it. Now it no longer showed, and when I opened the drawer I found the shirt-tail was loosely folded back.

It couldn't have been one of the staff; the maids at the Lamb finished work about lunch-time and, in any case, I doubted whether one of them would have taken the trouble to tuck the shirt away. I looked to see if anything was missing. It didn't take long, and as far as I could see nothing was; even the loose change I had left on the dressing-table because it was heavy in my trousers pocket was still there. So whoever had been in here, it wasn't a petty thief. But why should anybody else come into my room?

Yesterday evening an intruder had entered Laura's and my home, knocked out Nigel and escaped without taking anything. Now somebody had been in this room and left without taking anything. Surely it would be too much of a coincidence for there to be no connection between the two incidents? But what had he—or she, or they—wanted?

Turning, I noticed my brief-case lying where I had tossed it on the bed. This morning, a few minutes after Sapsed phoned her, Caroline Bedford had sent Millie Gant to ask me if I knew the whereabouts of the envelopes from Mrs. Sapsed's deed-box. A little while later, when I came down from coffee, Miss Bedford was in my room only two or three feet from my brief-case. She had denied that Sapsed had asked her to find the envelopes, but she could have been lying. Could have been, but why should she?

I doubted if it had been Sapsed at Cressford last night. And I couldn't see him risking coming here this evening; he was too well known in Lemsfield. So if the intruder had been looking for the envelopes on both occasions, either he had been acting for Sapsed or somebody else wanted them too.

Unlocking my case, I took them out and studied them again. Fourteen ordinary white envelopes with nothing remarkable or even interesting about them. I looked inside each one, but they were all empty. It was ridiculous to imagine anybody going to such lengths to recover them. Was I wrong after all, it was coincidence and no-one but Caroline Bedford was interested in them—and she only for the reason she had given me? Somehow I didn't think so.

Tucking the envelopes under the bottom sheet, I replaced the pillow and settled down to watch some television.

TEN

The phone rang. I picked it up.

"It's the Chief Inspector's office for you, Mr. Grierson," Cathy Pallett said.

I wondered without apprehension what the Chief's office wanted with me. Perhaps while I was in charge of the team, calls from them would be a regular feature of my life. It didn't inflate my ego too much.

"Mr. Grierson?" It was a woman's voice, instantly recognizable: Norma Witt, the Old Man's secretary.

"Yes," I said.

"Mr. Hudson would like to see you. As soon as possible. Can you make it today?"

I felt the first stirrings of uneasiness; there had been something slightly disturbing about that "as soon as possible."

"I think so," I agreed.

"There's a train from Lemsfield at eleven thirty-four."

The uneasiness became less vague. Norma might almost as well have added, "Be on it." The Old Man must want me up there pretty badly to get her to look up the trains. I was tempted to ask her if she knew what it was about, but she wouldn't tell me if she knew. She had been his secretary for more than ten years, and her discretion was a byword in the Department.

I looked up at the clock on the waiting-room wall. It said eleven ten. That didn't give me much time to do what I wanted. "I'll catch it," I said.

I did, with one minute to spare.

The train stopped once on the way and arrived at Euston at twelve forty-five. I walked through the gate at the end of the platform and straight on to the Underground station. Fortunately, King's Cross was on my way to the City, but it would mean my breaking my journey, and I hoped the Chief wasn't counting the minutes.

Platform Eight at King's Cross wore its customary air of grimily making do. Before leaving the branch, I had packed the wad of envelopes in a small box, wrapped the box in brown paper and labelled it "L. D. Stearn." I didn't expect anyone to search here for it, but if they did they were hardly likely to connect Laura's maiden name with me. I took it to the parcels office, deposited it and received a ticket in exchange. When I had done that, I walked back to the Underground feeling a good deal easier in my mind. I had chosen King's Cross because it was the London terminus for trains from Cressford and, just as important, not from Lemsfield. There was no reason why anybody looking for the parcel should search there any more than at Victoria or Waterloo.

George Hudson never felt any need to impress people by keeping them waiting unnecessarily, and within a couple of minutes of my presenting myself at the outer office I was facing him across the wide, uncluttered expanse of his desk. He didn't have a lot of papers on it to demonstrate that he worked hard, either; he knew he was secure in his reputation. Sitting there, waiting for him to say something, I tried to assess his mood from his expression and told myself that by this time I should know it was impossible; the Chinese had nothing on the Old Man when it came to inscrutability. Through the window behind him I could see a square of discoloured concrete across the street and, above it, a sliver of blue sky.

"You know why you're here?" It was a statement, rather

than a question, and his gruff, level tone sent my spirits several degrees lower. I knew now it wasn't to hear good news. More likely the opposite.

"No," I said truthfully.

He glared at me, uncertain whether I was playing the innocent or meant it. "There's been a complaint about you." He wasn't given to beating about the bush; you could take it or leave it.

I was startled. I wondered who had complained and what I had done, or not done, to offend them.

"I take it you know what I'm talking about now?"

"No."

He frowned. "The complaint came from a very high level. They spoke to the Chairman. You still tell me you don't know what it was about?"

"I've no idea," I said.

"Then, you're a bigger fool than I thought you were." If he was trying to get under my skin, to provoke me for some devious reasons of his own, he was near to succeeding. He leaned forward, thrusting his head towards me. "I warned you. I told you you were too fond of involving yourself in matters which had nothing to do with your job. Right?"

"Yes," I agreed. "And I haven't."

"What do you call it?" He was angry now; he probably suspected I was deliberately bandying words with him, and he didn't care if I saw it. Perhaps I was meant to. "Harassing a man whose wife has just been murdered. A Cabinet Minister with a crisis on his hands. What the hell did you think you were doing? I don't mind telling you, the Chairman's furious. The Bank's been made to look irresponsible. Probably malicious, too."

"If you're talking about Gerald Sapsed, I haven't harassed him," I said. "I've barely spoken to him."

"That's not the way he sees it."

"There's no other way to see it. I've hardly said twenty words to him in my life—and most of those were when he came to the branch with his wife's solicitor to open her deed-box. Her will was in it. Mr. Waites was there too, and Bates from E & T." I paused, satisfied I had made my point and he could hardly deny it. But I knew the Old Man well enough to understand that any feeling of triumph would be premature. "Did he complain, himself?"

"That doesn't matter. Luckily for you, they don't want any further action taken as far as you're concerned. But you're to be warned to behave yourself in future. I tell you, if I had my way it wouldn't stop there, you'd be out of the Department today."

"For doing what?" I demanded. I was really angry now. "Somebody rings up the Chairman and tells him a pack of lies and you take it for granted they're true. If somebody makes false statements about me behind my back I have a right to know who it is; I might want to talk to a solicitor."

For several seconds we eyed each other angrily. Then the Chief sat back in his chair and lowered his head in his favourite Churchillian attitude. Perhaps he expected me to wilt under that steady gaze; perhaps he was wondering if I was telling the truth.

"Why should anybody complain if it wasn't true?" he demanded less aggressively.

I had a good many ideas about that, none of which I could prove and none of them very plausible. Somebody must be badly worried to come out in the open and have me warned off. It had to be Sapsed—or somebody acting on his behalf. Somebody who operated at "a very high level," whatever that meant. But I wasn't ready to explain any of that to the Chief yet.

"I don't know," I admitted.

There was another longish silence; then he said, "Sapsed's account's at Lemsfield, isn't it?"

"Yes. I'm reporting his borrowings."

"Oh? Why?"

"I think we're at risk. I don't see how he can repay us."

The Old Man frowned. "His wife was pretty well off, wasn't she?"

"She left him a hundred pounds."

Stick that up your jumper, I thought. I wondered if the Chief played poker. I was prepared to bet he hadn't known about the terms of Rosemary Sapsed's will until that minute, but he didn't betray it by as much as a flicker of his eyelids. As soon as I had gone, he would be on the phone to Bates to find out where Mrs. Sapsed's money was going.

Silence again while he stared at me and thought.

"It's a police matter; is that clear? You're to have nothing to do with it unless you come across something that directly concerns the Bank. If that happens, you're to get in touch with John Parker or me. Especially, you're to do nothing which could possibly be construed as harassing Gerald Sapsed. Understood?"

"Yes, sir." I understood all right.

"Very well. I'll give you the benefit of the doubt this time, but I warn you, you'd better tread very carefully in future. Any more complaints and it'll be the finish as far as you're concerned." He paused; then, in a different tone, he asked, "How's the inspection going?"

"We should finish this week."

"What'll your report be like?"

"Good—with reservations. It's pretty clean."

The Chief grunted. "I was on the counter with Bob Waites at Leadenhall Street when we were both cashiers. He was a self-satisfied prig then. All right, you'd better get back. And don't forget what I've said."

I wasn't likely to.

The interview left me angry and resentful. The more I thought about it the more puzzled I became. Any large organization received occasional complaints about its staff or its services, many of them from cranks and trouble-makers or people with imagined grievances. This one was different. The Chief was no snob; when he said it had been made at a very high level he meant somebody with real authority. Somebody who could be put through to the Chairman and carried enough weight to make him act without, apparently, much in the way of question.

The Chief was usually a fair man, but he hadn't been interested in my side of the story. That suggested two things: that the source couldn't be doubted, what it said had to be accepted; and that it made no difference what I said in my defence, he had his instructions and they were to warn me off. True, in the end he had let me go with a caution, but the message was clear: I was to leave Sapsed alone and I was to take no interest in the manner of his wife's death.

The only person I knew who could have achieved that was Sapsed himself. But why should he want to? I had been telling the truth when I said I had exchanged barely twenty words with him. When I went to the house with Colin Bates I had left the talking to Bates; apart from some trite observation about the weather I had spoken only once, when I asked him if he knew anything about the envelopes in his wife's deed-box.

So I was back to them again. But why should my asking about them disturb Sapsed?

Of one thing I was certain: whoever complained had achieved the opposite of what he—or she—had intended. I was determined to find out why I had been warned off and by whom. With luck I could do so without even seeing the Minister.

I saw something else, sitting in a corner seat on the one fifty-seven train back to Lemsfield: that it might not be what I had already done which had alarmed somebody but what they believed I might do. In which case they must see me as a potential danger. Me, rather than the police? It was laughable. Unless—

Suddenly it wasn't funny any more; it was disturbing, almost frightening. Until this moment the lack of interest the police had shown in the intruder Nigel disturbed on Sunday evening had been irritating, but no more; now it seemed sinister. I knew the county police. It wasn't like them to shrug off an incident like that and suggest it had probably never happened. But if they had been instructed to do nothing by an authority they could not question—

Everything pointed to Sapsed as the murderer. He had had a motive—or believed he had, it amounted to the same thing —and he was the only person involved in the case with the power to pull strings like that. Authority at that level wouldn't have been persuaded to protect Carthy or Hillyer—nor the French girl, Monique Chabrier. She could have quarrelled with the dead woman, followed her to the wood and stabbed her, but the police must be satisfied she didn't or they would have arrested her by now.

Before parcelling up the envelopes, I had made a list of the figures on them. I took it out of my wallet now and studied it. As far as I could, I had copied the shape of the numbers. They were distinctive, the tops of the fours joined in neat triangles instead of being left open in the usual way and the sevens crossed with unusually long tails. Their angularity reminded me of the inscription on the photograph in Carthy's living-room.

The dates, if that was what they were, covered a period of nearly two years. Sometimes there was over two months between the nearest ones, sometimes only three weeks. Taking out my diary, I compared them with the last two years' calendars. There was no obvious pattern; the dates had not fallen on the same day of the week, for example, but they had all been Fridays, Saturdays or Sundays. Presumably, then, the money had been the fruits of some profitable weekend activity. Racing? Bridge? Sapsed was usually home at weekends.

But if that was the explanation, why lock the envelopes away in her deed-box? Gambling earnings weren't taxable. Had Rosemary Sapsed been like a squirrel, accumulating a hoard even when she had no need of the money? It seemed unlikely.

I put the list away in my wallet, and five minutes later the train pulled into Lemsfield.

When I got back to the bank, I went upstairs to the machine-room and looked out the dead woman's paid cheques. The fours and sevens had the same characteristics as those on the envelopes. There was nothing surprising in that, but it was confirmation.

Walking over to the trolleys on which were stacked the plastic trays of ledger sheets for the last few months, I found the one containing Sa to Se and flipped over the sheets until I came to Sapsed's. It was active for a personal account, and there were eight pages covering the four and a half months since the last year's sheets were taken out and bound. Six of the dates on my list were within that period, and on each of them Sapsed had drawn a substantial sum in cash.

I replaced the sheets and went downstairs to the book-room, a bleak cell lined with steel racks holding the bound ledger sheets for the last six or seven years. There was the familiar dry yet somehow musty odour of old paper. I found last year's ledger bearing the marking SAD–SLUT on its spine

—whoever did the binding had had to make it much fatter than usual to achieve that happy combination, and the one after it a good deal thinner—and turned to Gerald Baillie Sapsed. As on the other, more recent dates, those on the list corresponded with his drawing a large amount of cash. But in no case did the amount correspond with the sum in the envelope; it was always half as much again.

There must be a connection between them; it would be stretching coincidence too far to think there wasn't. It looked as if Sapsed had cashed the cheques, given his wife two thirds of the money and kept the rest for himself. For some reason, she had put her share in an envelope, dated it and deposited it in the box. But why? She was by far the wealthier of them and it was those heavy withdrawals which had led to Sapsed's debt to the Bank.

I remembered the expression I had seen on his face when the box was opened and he saw the neat layer of envelopes. He had been surprised, yes, but there was something more than that: horror.

I thought now I knew why. The idea seemed so preposterous I could hardly believe it, but I was convinced it was the truth. No wonder Sapsed had been desperate to recover the envelopes.

I replaced the ledger on the shelf, switched off the light and went back upstairs to the waiting-room.

ELEVEN

Rosemary Sapsed had been blackmailing her husband.

No wonder, when Wheatley opened her deed-box and he saw the envelopes, Sapsed looked as if he had seen a ghost. Probably he had put the money in them and sealed them himself. Almost certainly he had; he wouldn't have trusted anyone else to do it. I remembered his tortured "Oh, God!" Had he understood then, for the first time perhaps, how much his wife had hated him?

She hadn't spent the money, she hadn't needed it; the extortion, in the most painful way she could conceive, had been everything. Why? Because it satisfied some need, some dark, sadistic streak in her? There seemed something appallingly calculated about the dates on the envelopes now; they were like the dates with which a butterfly collector might label his specimens after trapping and killing them, only infinitely worse.

Martyn Carthy had called her a bitch and said she hated Sapsed and was trying to destroy him. At the time, I had put it down to the drink talking, but perhaps it had been more than that. Surely he hadn't known about the blackmail?

If she hadn't needed the money, why had she opened the envelopes? To make sure the money was there and gloat over it? Perhaps.

Sapsed had been the victim, but he wasn't wholly innocent himself. For blackmail to succeed, the victim had to possess a guilty secret—one he dared not have revealed—that was the essence of the whole vicious, sordid business. What was Sapsed's secret?

I told myself I neither knew nor cared. If his wife had been blackmailing him and he had killed her I wouldn't approve, but I would prefer not to know the nature of the hold she had over him. At least now I understood why he had wanted me warned off; he couldn't risk anybody asking questions.

But it wasn't as simple as that. He had been prepared to use the power he possessed to protect himself. Perhaps he believed he could control the police, at least while the NATO crisis lasted and the country needed him. For so long, people even more powerful than he was would support him, but a meddling nobody like me blundering about might stumble on the truth almost inadvertently. So he had had my house searched on Sunday evening and, when the envelopes weren't found there, my room at the Lamb the next evening.

It was ironic that, until the complaint of my harassing him, I had probably taken less interest in the murder than most people in Lemsfield. I had wondered about the envelopes, but my real concern had been Sapsed's ability to repay the Bank.

If I ignored the warning I had been given I would be asking for trouble. Not only would I be thrown out of the Department; in all likelihood I would lose my job. Sapsed held all the aces. How could I hope to confront the forces who would rally to his support and emerge unscathed? I wasn't even sure I wanted to.

The doubts didn't last long. My house had been entered, a friend assaulted, my room searched and allegations which were untrue made about me. I had to do something.

First, I walked round to the public library. The air in the Ridings smelt of petrol fumes and heat. Young mothers who looked as if they were being tried to the limits of their endurance dragged by the hand grizzling, unhappy children. I wondered how much longer the heat wave would last before it blew up in a violent storm.

The reference library was on the first floor. I found a fairly recent edition of Who's Who and carried it over to a table which was unoccupied. Gerald Baillie Sapsed had been educated at a minor public school and Cambridge. From 1963 to 1967 he had been a lecturer in economics at the University of Wessex. In 1969 he had taken a post at Conservative Central Office and, shortly afterwards, been adopted as a prospective candidate. Elected at the next general election, he had worked his way steadily up the political ladder: parliamentary private secretary, junior minister, shadow spokesman on trade, then on defence. He had been appointed to his present job just over a year ago.

The bare outline of a man's life. The facts were there, but they told me nothing about him. I wanted to make a telephone call, a confidential call, and the waiting-room at the bank was hardly the place to do that; people were liable to walk in without ceremony and, although I had no reason for supposing Cathy Pallett wasn't trustworthy, she might inadvertently hear something I would rather she didn't. I walked back towards the bank, crossed the street and entered the post office. The two phone boxes were unoccupied. I went into the one farther from the queues at the counter, pulled the heavy door to behind me and looked in my diary for the number of Jack Catlow's paper.

Catlow was a journalist. We had known each other for nearly two years and helped each other more than once; I hoped he would be able to help me now.

The switchboard put me through to him, and for a minute or two we exchanged the usual pleasantries, before he asked, "What can I do for you?" I explained and heard him whistle softly. "You're into the big league now, aren't you?"

"Bigger," I agreed.

"I'll see what I can do, but don't expect miracles; it could be tricky. Where shall I ring you?"

"It'd be better if you didn't," I told him. "Can I give you a call in the morning?"

"If you say so."

We said goodbye, and I walked out into the street. The air still stank of petrol fumes. I returned to the bank, shut myself in the waiting-room and took the remaining staff reports from my brief-case. The top one was Caroline Bedford's, and I read the first page curiously. As far as I could see, she had had no connections with the district until she was transferred to Lemsfield, eighteen months before. She had been born in Hampshire and joined the staff as a graduate entrant when she was twenty-one. It was clear from her progress since then that she was being groomed as star material: a spell abroad with Overseas Division, two brief attachments to head office departments and, I was surprised to see, a year on Inspection; she had left just before I joined the Department. If she didn't blot her copybook she wouldn't be Waites' assistant manager much longer. And then? Well, she was thirty-three and probably more interested in her career than in marriage and children. She could end up in some very senior job indeed.

I glanced through the other reports, then went to find Stephanie Fortune, the first cashier, who was next on my list. She was an efficient, attractive girl of twenty-seven, and we chatted about her work until something she said reminded me of Sapsed and I asked her if he often came to the bank.

"Not very," she answered.

"Do you like him?"

Stephanie almost shrugged. "He's all right. He's quite friendly and that, but he doesn't say much."

"What was she like?"

This time Stephanie hesitated. "She was always pleasant enough when she came in, but—"

"But what?" I prompted her, curious.

"I don't know really. Sometimes she looked as if she could be a proper bitch. It was something about her; she seemed all strung up and on edge. As if she'd boil over if you said something she didn't like. It wasn't often."

I reflected that Stephanie appeared to have been more perceptive than most people who had known the dead woman. "Do you know Martyn Carthy?" I asked her.

"Not really. Ivor does."

"Ivor?"

"My husband; he's on the Conservative Club committee. Poor Martyn." Stephanie laughed.

"Why poor?"

"Do you know him? And he had it badly for Mrs. Sapsed."

I remembered the photograph in his flat and something Mrs. Henderson had said that evening when Waites introduced me to her and her husband. It was after Carthy had left us, something about his not being able to stand Hillyer. She had laughed too, like Stephanie. And Rosemary Sapsed had left nearly everything she possessed to Hillyer.

Carthy might be a good agent—presumably he was, however surprising that might be—but there was something slightly pathetic about him. I couldn't see a woman like Rosemary Sapsed returning his affection; he was too spineless. More likely she had used him mercilessly and laughed at him behind his back. If he had been in love with her, a man like Carthy would have suffered miserably, tormented by guilt and divided loyalties. And if she had rejected him for Hillyer it would explain his hating the farmer.

If she had laughed at him, he might have killed her. What was it Wilde wrote? "Each man kills the thing he loves, the brave man with a sword." It hadn't been a sword that killed Mrs. Sapsed, but a knife was not so different. Love—infatuation, even—turned to hatred could be a powerful destructive force.

I tried to picture Carthy, quiet, ineffectual outside his work, loyal to Sapsed and in love with his wife. Then rejected, perhaps humiliated. Oh, he could have killed her all right. But did he? And although he might have invented some cock-and-bull story to persuade Sapsed to use his influence and have me warned off, I couldn't see him having my house searched and the police coerced. Sapsed was the only one who could have done that.

Perhaps he had asked for no more than recognition of his existence and a kind word now and then; the Martyn Carthys of the world thrive on hopeless causes. Especially their own.

"There's another customer who comes into the Lamb," I said. "A farmer named Hillyer."

"Oh, him," Stephanie responded.

"Why 'Oh, him'?"

"He's useless. He drinks too much and he's up to his ears in debt."

"Is he married?"

"Not now. He was divorced three or four years ago; his wife runs a stables."

I doubted if there was anything more she could tell me, and I was afraid of seeming too interested in the Sapseds and their circle. We talked for a little longer; then she went back to the counter and sent the next person on my list to see me.

By the time I finished work, there were only a few people still to see, among them Caroline Bedford and Waites. I told myself it would be a mistake to interview Miss Bedford while she was still so hostile, but I knew I was deceiving myself and that the real reason for my putting off seeing her was the ambivalence of my own feelings. She both antagonized and attracted me—and I wasn't ready to face that yet.

The *Star* had a new story on its front page that evening: a student at the Polytechnic named Andrew Garvie was at the police station helping the police with their inquiries. According to the report, he was prominent in extreme Left-wing politics at the Poly and had played a leading rôle in the demonstration outside the civic hall. I wondered if the police really believed he had killed Rosemary Sapsed. If they knew anything more than was in the *Star* they would keep it to themselves. Did they know she had been blackmailing her husband?

Tucking the paper under my arm, I went up to my room. The maid had left the window open and a pleasant little breeze stirred the curtains. The feel of it on my skin made me realize how hot and sticky I was, and I stripped off my clothes and turned on the shower.

After the shower I felt better. I dressed again and went down to the bar. It was nearly deserted and there was nobody I knew amongst the three or four customers. I asked Danny for a half of bitter and helped myself to some nuts.

After dinner I decided to go for a walk. I would have preferred to go swimming, but that was hardly practicable after the meal I had just eaten, and anyway the pool would be crowded. Outside the hotel I turned right, leaving the Old Town and walking down the hill, past the undistinguished houses, built in the twenties and thirties, which now constituted a sort of no man's land, a buffer between the Old Town and the brashness of the Ridings. Away to the right, between the river and the main London road, the concrete and glass blocks of the Polytechnic buildings stood up square and aggressive against the azure blue sky. Behind them, green darkening almost to black, rose the wooded slopes on the other side of the valley with, at their foot, the garish red and yellow signs of a petrol station little more than pin-points of light.

There was a fairly constant stream of traffic in both directions, but not many people walked this way in the evenings, and once when, for no particular reason, I glanced behind me, there was only one person in sight. It was a man and he was some way back, but I was pretty sure it was Roberts, the new arrival at the Lamb. He had probably had the same idea: a walk, then one or two drinks in the bar and watch the news before going to bed. It was an exciting life.

I turned right again, past the court building and the police station and walked on until I came to the river. It was at its narrowest here, barely a dozen feet wide, and overhung in places by fine old trees. I passed two small boys sailing a boat and met a couple, arms round each other's waist, the girl leaning against the boy. Somewhere in the distance there was shouting, but it was too far away to be intelligible.

Leaving the river, I headed back towards the Ridings. The man who had been behind me was still there, a little closer now. It was strange he should have taken the same round-about route I had, and I walked on with a vague sense of foreboding.

The shouting was louder now, a rhythmic chanting. Oh no! I thought. Surely history couldn't be repeating itself so soon.

Posters outside the civic hall announced future pro-grammes: rock music and symphony concerts, the local oper-atic society's production of *Iolanthe* and a charity boxing din-ner. This evening it was wrestling, and a few people were trickling through the doors where, just over a week ago, Sapsed and his wife had emerged to find a hostile crowd wait-ing. This evening there were more women than men, most of them middle-aged or elderly. For them, I supposed, wrestling was a change from bingo, housey-housey with simulated vio-lence.

Eight days ago I had stood here and watched the crowd pushing and shoving and the police struggling to hold it back. Later I had listened to Mrs. Sapsed calling the demonstrators a rabble. Had she spoken as she had deliberately, knowing the resentment her words would cause, and that some of it would harm her husband? A mind devious enough to resort to blackmail to relieve its hatred would surely be capable of that.

And now Rosemary Sapsed was dead.

With every step I took, the shouting grew louder and nearer. I reached the pavement and turned right towards the bottom end of the Ridings. As I did so, a crowd erupted round a corner a couple of hundred yards away. There must have been at least two hundred of them, waving placards and chanting. I could distinguish the words now, although they were still too far off for me to read the slogans painted on their banners. "Free Garvie. Down with pigs. Free Garvie. Down with pigs." It was repeated over and over again until the words lost any meaning and the chanting became a mindless ritual.

Most of the crowd were young men, but there were some girls among them and a few older people. Some of their faces were angry, burning with the fires of fanaticism, and I was reminded of the expressions I had seen that other evening. Some looked happy, laughing, as if to those few it was all a joke. They came up the Ridings, marching, raggedly, it was true, but in some semblance of order. Despite the shouting and the anger on many of their faces, there was nothing particularly menacing about them.

Or so it seemed to me. But then, suddenly, the whole picture changed. A group thirty or forty strong who had been standing on the pavement across the street from me, apparently just watching, charged at the marchers. Some of them waved Union Jacks, a few had sticks. As they surged forward, people who were standing near them were swept along, helpless. Within seconds, what had been a peaceful demonstration had become much more like a pitched battle. Brawling groups broke away from the main conflict, staggering and rolling in the road. Men shouted curses and women screamed.

I felt a heavy blow in the middle of my back and staggered, losing my footing as I went over the edge of the pavement and nearly falling. I fought to stay upright; anyone falling to the ground would be lucky to escape injury, probably serious, amidst those milling, trampling feet. Something hard, I guessed it was the staff of a banner, struck my right shoulder, sending pain shooting down my arm, then numbing it. I pushed and shoved, myself, trying to get clear of the scrum around me.

A yard away a young woman had been caught up as I had. Her back was to me, but I could see her striving desperately to get away from the mob. The end of a thick stick, swung viciously at anything within range, struck her across the shoulder-blades and she fell. There was only one person between us, a gangling youth with a skin-head haircut and an earring in his left ear shouting obscenities and waving his fists with an ecstatic look on his face. I wrapped my left arm round his chest, pressed my right knee in the lower part of his back and heaved. He came backwards fast, gurgling. I let go, and as he went past me I saw the surprise in his eyes.

The girl was on all fours, trying to pull herself upright. I bent down, put my hands under her armpits and dragged her to her feet. She gasped something, but there was too much noise for me to hear what it was.

The skin-head was coming for me, surprise replaced by blind fury. I saw him start to raise his right arm and something glitter in his hand. Without waiting to see what it was, I drove my right knee up into the pit of his stomach with all the strength I could muster. He grunted, doubled up and fell back against the heaving bodies behind him. The girl's back was still to me; I grasped her arm and dragged her out of the mêlée.

Two policemen were running towards us, and I could hear sirens wailing in the distance. It was no place to hang around. Pulling the girl after me, I began to run towards the civic hall, a hundred yards away.

She was panting hard, gasping for breath. Half-way there I saw a shop doorway with a porch and dragged her into its comparative shelter. Only then did I stop to look at her.

"You!" Caroline Bedford exclaimed, choking a little over the words.

We stared at each other. There was just sufficient light in the porch for me to see her eyes wide with shock or fear and a nasty-looking cut on her forehead. Her dress was torn too.

"Are you all right?" I asked her. She nodded. "We'd better get out of this."

She didn't look too steady on her feet, and as I put my hand on her arm and urged her forward she staggered slightly. I put my arm around her waist to support her. I could feel her soft, firm flesh through the thin dress she was wearing, but she must have been too tired, or too frightened, to say anything; she let my hand stay there.

"Where do you live?" I asked.

There was a noticeable pause before she answered. Either she was still out of breath or she was considering the alternatives; she wanted to be rid of my company, but at the same time she didn't feel like walking home alone.

"Finchley Court," she said so quietly I hardly heard it. "It's in Lowmoor."

It would be, I told myself. Lowmoor was on the other side of the river, a village which had been engulfed in the tide of the New Town. Finchley Court could be anything from half a mile to three times that distance from the Ridings. Then I remembered I had seen taxis standing outside the civic hall; perhaps there was a rank there. Or, at least, we might find one hanging around.

Nobody followed us, those people who had found themselves caught up in the fracas against their will had evidently decided discretion was the better part of valour. Once, looking back, I saw the intermittent flashing blue lights of two police cars.

They hadn't wasted any time; it was only a few minutes since the fighting had started.

TWELVE

I was glad we had taken a taxi, Finchley Court was over a mile from the Ridings and up a fairly steep hill; Lowmoor was a misnomer. Caroline Bedford's flat was on the fifth floor, the top. I wondered why the people I was landed with taking home always lived at the top of buildings.

Despite the taxi, by the time we reached her landing she looked as if she had had more than enough for one evening. Maybe the blow on her head had been worse than I thought. She let me take her key with no more than a token protest, and I helped her inside and into an easy-chair in the living-room. The block was modern without being aggressively so: brick walls, not concrete; and landings that didn't look as if they had been modelled on a gaol. Her living-room was furnished in slightly negative good taste, prints of Canalettos and Turners on the walls, a settee and an easy-chair with brown upholstery, a bookcase, and a dining-table and four chairs in the window. I imagined her giving pretentious little dinner parties for other graduates who, like her, felt superior to the people with whom they worked; evenings of prissy food, bad wine and affected conversation. All the same, it was a pleasant, airy room and it had the appearance of a place where somebody lived.

"Where's your kitchen?" I asked her.

"Through there." She nodded weakly at a door in the opposite wall.

I walked through, found a glass and half filled it with water.

When I took it back to her, she murmured her thanks. The door across the hall was her bedroom. I saw a single bed, neat unfussy things, shut the door again quickly and tried the one farther along. This time it was the bathroom. There was a flannel on a hook over the basin; I soaked it in cold water and took it back to the living-room. Water dripped on to the floor but I couldn't help that.

Miss Bedford was studying the cut on her forehead in a small mirror.

"We'll be able to see it better when you've cleaned it up," I said.

"Yes." She took the flannel and wiped away the congealed blood. The cut had stopped bleeding some time ago, and when she had cleaned it, it looked better—almost trivial. I suspected there was more bruising than open wound and wondered what had caused it, a stick or one of those milling feet.

"Perhaps you ought to go to hospital. Just to let them have a look," I suggested.

She shook her head, making herself wince. "I told you, I'm all right. It's nothing much."

"Okay."

She returned the mirror to her handbag and looked up at me. I was surprised to see her face was slightly flushed with embarrassment. "I'm sorry about yesterday lunch-time."

"So am I," I said. It probably sounded more like an apology than it was intended to be. I was sorry because she had walked out on me without telling me what I wanted to know and, more, because she had made me feel boorish. I wouldn't have pressed her now if she hadn't insisted she was all right. "The Chief sent for me this morning. Somebody had complained to the Chairman I was harassing Sapsed."

Her eyes met mine, then looked away. Her cheeks were still pink, and if I hadn't known it couldn't have been her I might have wondered, she looked so guilty.

"Do you know who it was?" she asked.

"I can guess."

"Who?" She was tense now.

"Somebody who could speak to the Chairman personally and carried a lot of weight. Somebody like Sapsed."

A frown puckered her forehead. "Were you harassing him?"

"I haven't spoken more than about twenty words to him in my life and I haven't phoned him. That doesn't sound like harassment to me."

"Then, why should he complain?"

"That's what I'd like to know." I sat down on the arm of the easy-chair facing her.

"Why are you telling me?"

"I thought you might be able to guess who it was. You and Sapsed are friends, aren't you?"

There was the slightest of pauses before she answered, "Hardly that. I know him; he's a customer." She said it levelly, as if picking her words carefully.

"You knew him before you came here," I said. "A long time ago, didn't you?"

"What gives you that idea?"

"You were at Wessex University between 1964 and 1967; Sapsed was an economics lecturer there then."

"A university's a big place; there were eight thousand students at Wessex when I was there. You see lots of people without knowing them." The challenge was back in her lovely eyes, but she was still on guard.

"You were reading economics," I said. "Why did you ask for a move here? I wouldn't have thought Lemsfield was your sort of place. Not enough intellectual company."

"Is it any business of yours?" Her tone was cool, mildly interested, not angry.

I nodded. "Yes, for two reasons. First, if it affects your work or the Bank, second, because since I came here somebody has complained about my doing something I haven't done, my house has been broken into and a friend attacked, and last night my room at the Lamb was searched. I'm pretty sure I was followed this evening, too. And all that has something to do with your friend Sapsed."

"You sound as if you're becoming paranoid."

"Only, I'm not imagining any of it; it all happened."

"You would say that, wouldn't you? People always do when they're imagining things."

"When they're unbalanced, you mean?"

"You said it, I didn't."

"Would you like me to ring the neighbour who was laid out?"

Caroline Bedford shrugged. "Certainly, if it would make you feel any better." She paused. "All right, you say it happened; what has it got to do with me?"

"Why did Sapsed want those envelopes?" I had shot the question at her, hoping to take her off guard, but she answered scathingly.

"You're not back to that again!"

"His wife was blackmailing him."

Miss Bedford stared at me, and, for a few seconds, time seemed to stand still. Then she said, "You must be mad."

"That's why he was so shocked when he saw the envelopes in her deed-box. He was afraid somebody might start asking questions. You saw him and nearly passed out."

"Your imagination again."

"No. He had me warned off, not because of anything I'd done already but what he was afraid I might do. You told him I'd got the envelopes, didn't you?"

"No. You told Millie you hadn't."

"Not quite. I said I couldn't help you." I didn't believe her; it was the only way Sapsed could have known where they were. "That's why he killed her, isn't it? Because she was blackmailing him. But afterwards he couldn't afford to have people know she was, because it gave him a motive. And a man in his position mustn't be open to blackmail."

"My God, you've an imagination," Caroline Bedford exclaimed.

"You're good at your job and you assess any proposition carefully before you agree to lend, yet you allowed Sapsed to borrow more and more without seeing any estimates or receipts or even checking if he'd really had any work done to the house. From what you say, you didn't even find out it wasn't his; it was in his wife's name. You knew he really needed the money to pay her. He wouldn't have told anyone; there has to be a reason why he told you."

Caroline stood up. I saw her sway very slightly, but she regained control of herself immediately, and when she spoke, her tone was biting. "I'm grateful to you for bringing me home, but that doesn't give you the right to keep me sitting here listening to your innuendoes. I'm going to bed now; will you shut the door behind you when you leave."

"I'll go," I said. "You realize that if there is anything between you and Sapsed and the police find out, you'll be under suspicion, don't you? And don't kid yourself they won't find out."

She stared at me as if I had voiced a fear which had been tormenting her for days. "They've arrested a student," she said dully. "That's what the demo was about."

"They haven't arrested him, they're just asking him some questions. The rest of the students over-reacted because they wanted to have a go at the police."

Again Caroline looked at me, then away before she spoke. "All right," she said, "Gerald and I have been lovers for a long time. Now you know."

"I'm not interested in what you do." Bloody liar, I thought. I was shocked to realize how much I did care.

"You may as well know, you've guessed anyway. It started when I was at Wessex. It didn't last long then, but we met again by accident nearly two years ago. We had dinner together and Gerald told me his marriage hadn't worked out. I didn't know then what Rosemary was really like."

"What was she like?" I asked.

The grey eyes met mine. "Don't you know? She was warped, unbalanced. She was trying to ruin Gerald because he was successful. I don't know, perhaps she couldn't help it. She used to make up nasty little stories about him and tell them to people; anything to belittle him."

"Did he know who it was blackmailing him?"

"No. That's why he was so shocked when he saw the envelopes. And he couldn't go to the police; he couldn't have anyone see he could be blackmailed. You were right about that."

"Did he tell you what he was being blackmailed about?" I asked.

"Can't you guess?" Caroline sounded surprised.

"You?"

"Yes. Do you think that made me feel any better?"

Probably not, I thought. "How was it done?"

"He used to get telephone calls when he was at his flat in London, telling him how much and where to leave it. I was there once."

"Didn't he recognize her voice?"

"It wasn't her; it was always a man."

Sapsed must have trusted Caroline to tell her so much, I reflected. He would have had no qualms about asking her to recover the envelopes. She was holding a fragile glass ornament, a thin, elegant heron, and suddenly I heard a tiny crack. She looked down at the two pieces in her hands.

"Gerald didn't kill her," she said.

"How do you know?" But I hadn't needed to ask; I knew the answer before she spoke.

"He was with me."

Quite calmly, she walked out to the kitchen. I heard the pedal bin open, then the gentle thud as it closed again. When she returned, she was wiping her hands together.

"How well does Sapsed know Peter Hillyer?" I asked her.

She looked surprised. "Not very well, as far as I know. He can't stand him."

That was only to be expected; even if the Minister hadn't known about Hillyer's friendship with his wife, they were very different, antagonistic types. "Was Hillyer having an affair with Mrs. Sapsed?"

The question appeared to startle Caroline; Sapsed couldn't have told her about his wife's will yet. "I don't know," she said. "I hadn't thought—"

She could have been lying to protect Sapsed, because if he had known, it provided him with another motive for killing Rosemary, but her surprise had looked genuine. Yet for a woman of Rosemary Sapsed's temperament, surely part of the enjoyment of the affair would have been in having a lover whom her husband detested. Wouldn't she have made sure he knew about it? Not that that necessarily meant he would have told Caroline.

"When did you last see Sapsed?" I asked her.

"That morning when he came to the bank. Friday."

I thought that was probably the truth. Sapsed wouldn't have risked being seen with her just now. "But he did ring you and ask what had happened to the envelopes?"

Caroline nodded. "Yes."

It was what I had wanted, her confirmation of that. Now I had it, there was no point in my staying any longer. She didn't need me. I stood up.

"I'll go now," I told her. "You're sure you'll be all right?"

"Yes, of course."

She must have wanted it to sound confident, even angry, but it came out uncertain and a little frightened. We turned at the same moment and somehow came close, facing each other. She looked up at me and I saw the doubt and fear in her eyes. Her lips were trembling slightly and, almost without thinking, I put my arm round her reassuringly.

"Look—" I said.

The next moment she was in my arms, her head pressed against my shoulder, fighting back the tears. I could feel her fingers gripping my arms, kneading the flesh with a sort of desperation, and I knew then what I had refused to admit before, even to myself, that I wanted her.

We stayed like that for perhaps a quarter of a minute, then she gave a long, shuddering sigh and moved away a little. Her eyes were bright through the unshed tears, and a tremulous little smile touched the corners of her lips. I kissed them, without calculation, as if it were inevitable I should, and she responded, pressing herself against me as if by doing so she could extinguish her fears.

This time when she moved away she avoided my eyes. "I'm sorry," she muttered.

"What for?"

With a trace of her old prickliness she demanded, "I suppose you think I'm just a weak, silly girl who needs a man to comfort her?"

"Not particularly," I said. "Not weak and silly, anyhow. We all need comforting sometimes. But that wasn't why I kissed you."

"Then, why did you?" It was a challenge.

"Because I wanted to and—"

"And what?"

"You know why." It sounded harsher than I had intended it to.

She said, "Oh," like a startled child.

"Why did you kiss me back?"

"You aren't supposed to ask questions like that."

"No," I agreed.

She turned away, and for a moment neither of us spoke. Her right hand played with a corner of a cushion. Then she said, "Gerald didn't kill her; he was with me." She paused. "People say all murderers are mad, don't they? Do you believe that?"

"I don't know." I thought of the few I had known—or thought at the time I had known. They had seemed normal enough, but who knew what went on inside them?

"Perhaps there's something lacking in them, something other people have. Or perhaps it's the other way round and they have too much of something."

"Perhaps," I agreed. "But it seems to me murder's the ultimate selfishness. I don't mean killing when the person's driven beyond the limits of his endurance, but murder for gain or one's own safety."

"I hadn't thought of it like that," Caroline said, sounding surprised. Then she added in a different tone, "Must you go yet?"

"I'm afraid so." It wasn't true; I didn't have to go—had nowhere to go but back to the Lamb to drink or watch television by myself—and I would rather have stayed, but I knew I should. That if I didn't I would be sorry later.

"All right, if you must. Goodbye, David, and thank you."

For a second or two we stood there looking at each other. Perhaps neither of us was sure whether we should kiss again, whether the other wanted it. It was Caroline who made the move, she kissed me quickly and warmly and stepped back.

"Goodbye," I said.

I knew she was still standing there looking after me as I walked into the hall and let myself out. I crossed the landing to the lift and, when it came, got in, pressed the button and went down to the lobby.

By now I knew my way about Lemsfield well enough to be fairly confident that if I walked up the hill to the T-junction at the top, turned left there and continued for a quarter of a mile or so, I would come to another road which would take me back over the river to the Old Town. If I was right, it would be three quarters of a mile shorter that way than going the way we had come in the taxi.

The lift stopped at the ground floor, the door slid open and I stepped out. Light still filtered in through the double swing-doors. Enough for me to see the two men. One of them, in uniform, was a stranger, the other was the new arrival at the hotel, Roberts.

"You are David Grierson?" the uniformed one asked me.

I was filled with a sudden sense of foreboding. "Yes," I admitted.

They must have been waiting for me. Why? And what was Roberts doing here? My conscience was clear—legally, at least —but that didn't help much.

"I must ask you to come with us." The uniformed police-man was young and looked hard. His fair hair protruded thickly from under his cap and he had the sort of lanky frame which would put on weight fast in another ten years.

"Why?" I demanded.

"I have reason to believe you were involved in an affray earlier this evening."

I didn't like it. If they wanted me to be a witness it seemed a strange way to go about it.

"I wasn't involved," I said. "At least, only by accident." I glanced at Roberts, who was standing there looking watchful and unsympathetic. "Who are you?"

Neither of them answered.

"Look—" I began. I might as well have addressed a brick wall, for all the response I got.

"Just come along with us," the uniformed one said.

I hadn't much choice. They led me out to their car and saw me into the back. Roberts climbed in beside me.

The police station was large, modern and about as homely as Dartmoor. Or that was how it seemed to me. I was taken to a small, bare room with a table, two chairs and not much else and charged that on that evening I had behaved in a manner likely to cause a breach of Her Majesty's peace and, for good measure, with assaulting a male person, name unknown, thereby causing him actual bodily harm. Roberts must have seen me dealing with the skin-head.

"I was rescuing a woman who had been knocked down," I protested. "That's all. Ask her."

"You'll have a chance to put your side in court," they said. By this time, "they" was a burly sergeant who had the air of one who had heard it all so many times before he no longer believed anything. There couldn't be many jobs calculated to instil cynicism more thoroughly, I thought.

I endured the formalities resentfully, trying not to let my anger show, because I knew it wouldn't do any good and might do a lot of harm. When I asked to see a solicitor, they said, "Later." I wondered how much later and tried to remember all I had ever been told about the rights of accused persons. It wasn't much, because I had never expected to be one and hadn't taken much notice.

I asked about bail. Apparently that was something else which had to wait for the court to pronounce. I didn't believe it, but there wasn't much I could do.

In the end, they took me downstairs and put me in a cell.

THIRTEEN

It was the first time I had seen a cell, let alone been locked in one. The experience was humiliating first and infuriating second. Perhaps if I had been guilty I might have accepted it with more resignation. As it was, I threw myself down on the hard, narrow bed and raged inwardly with silent, impotent fury. I was too angry to be sorry for myself. Then I decided that was getting me nowhere and started trying to think more constructively. You get plenty of time to think locked up in a cell by yourself, and with nothing else to do I thought a good deal.

Presumably somebody would let the Bank know where I was eventually. I could picture Waites' expression when he heard: fastidious distaste. Ben and Trevor would be concerned but, I suspected, half-amused too. One of them would tell district office and they in turn would let Inspection at head office know. I preferred not to think what Hudson would say. He was unlikely to look kindly on one of his staff appearing in court charged with assault and a breach of the peace, not even if I was acquitted—and I knew enough about the workings of courts not to take that for granted. Whatever the naïve and innocent-minded might believe, courts meted out the law, not justice, and the two could be very different. I wasn't deluding myself Roberts wouldn't perjure himself without turning a hair if it suited his purpose. For Roberts, I knew now without the slightest doubt, was one of "them."

Who were "they?" Not the ordinary police. More likely the

Special Branch. Weren't they responsible for protecting members of the government? They could have seen that the local police took only a token interest in what had happened at Laura's and my house on Sunday evening. A word at a high level to the chief constable would have ensured that.

High level. The Chief had said the complaint about me had come at a very high level. The clans were rallying to protect their own.

I was pretty sure Roberts had followed me from the Lamb this evening. No doubt he had seen me get into the taxi with Caroline. Sapsed must have confessed to his involvement with her to explain the importance of recovering the envelopes, and Roberts would have known where she lived. But why had he arranged for me to be arrested?

It was two or three minutes before I saw the answer: somebody had wanted me out of the way.

Why? I would know no less when I was allowed to return to circulation than I did now. Something must be planned for while I was incarcerated here. What was it?

I went over and over it in my mind, trying to arrange all I knew into a logical pattern. The seconds ticked by and became minutes, but an hour was eternity. Involved in a Kafka-esque nightmare, I was developing a split personality: what was happening didn't concern the real me, but somebody else. Soon I would resume my true identity and return to my normal, fairly humdrum existence, and it would be as though the nightmare had never happened.

My thoughts wandered, and for a while I almost forgot Sapsed, his wife and all that had happened during the past week. Then, perhaps because I was no longer thinking about it, the answer came and I knew why I was there. On Sunday night Nigel had disturbed an intruder in our house and been knocked out. Whoever attacked him could have been there only a short time, because Diane had seen the Capri draw up when she went out to collect her children's toys. Then he—Roberts?—had heard me coming and fled. He had been looking for the envelopes, and he hadn't found them because they were in my brief-case in the Triumph, but he didn't know that.

The next evening somebody—Roberts again?—had searched my room at the Lamb, again without success. Now they wanted me out of the way while they made a more thorough search. I guessed they had already made sure I hadn't deposited the envelopes at the bank.

I was thankful I had told nobody there about my summons to head office. Unless they had been watching me then, they would have no way of knowing about my going to King's Cross—and if they had, there would have been no need for this charade. For the first time since leaving Caroline's flat I felt a glow of satisfaction. The envelopes were safe, and now I knew they or, rather, what they represented—Sapsed's vulnerability to blackmail—was the key to it all.

Except the murder itself. I was still convinced he hadn't suspected his wife was the blackmailer until he saw the envelopes in her deed-box.

Why hadn't he gone to the police when the blackmail started? True, however hopefully the courts promised anonymity the truth almost invariably leaked out and the victim suffered as much as, perhaps more than, the blackmailer. Even so, in these permissive days there wouldn't have been too great a scandal. Sapsed might have slipped a little in the estimation of some of his constituents, but there was unlikely to be a general election for another three years at least and the public's memory was notoriously short. It certainly wasn't that he cared enough for his wife to want to save her from being hurt by learning about Caroline Bedford.

I was very tired. After a while I slept fitfully and woke unrefreshed. A policeman brought me breakfast. I was surprised to find I was hungry and the food was a lot tastier than I had expected.

Later, a lot later, there were sounds of movement in the passage outside my cell, a key rattled in the lock and the door was thrown open. The same jailer appeared in the doorway and I could see another outside.

"Come on," the first one told me. His tone was a subtle blend of resignation and tolerance; he had seen it all before and expected to see it hundreds of times in the future. I was just a statistic, one more in the endless procession of people who passed through his hands. My guilt or innocence meant nothing to him.

With two others, a squat, dirty old man with tangled hair and a three-day stubble who smelt, and a thin, consumptive-looking youth who looked so guilty he was probably innocent, I was escorted up the stairs and out through the back of the police station to a yard. There we were loaded into a van for the hundred-yard drive to the court building. At least it was better than being led through the streets in handcuffs, I told myself. It wasn't much consolation.

Another cell, no better and no worse than the first. I repeated that I wanted to see a solicitor and again they told me, "Later."

Time dragged on slowly, as before. My case was the last to be heard. I wondered if there was any significance in that, if they were deliberately delaying my appearance to give them as long as possible. Then, at last, in mid-afternoon, I was taken into the court room.

It was quite small, modern and bare. I suppose that, without really thinking about it, I had expected it to be crowded, but, apart from the magistrate, his clerk and a handful of policemen, it was almost empty. There was nobody from the Bank. That, at least, was a relief. The strange sensation that I was taking part in a charade which had no relevance for me returned.

When the clerk asked me how I pleaded I replied, "Not guilty," with less vehemence than I had intended and said yet again that I wanted to see a solicitor. The magistrate looked across at the uniformed inspector who was prosecuting for the police, a youngish, efficient-looking man.

"We've not been able to contact his solicitor, sir," he reported.

"I didn't ask for any particular solicitor, just a solicitor," I said.

The magistrate regarded me thoughtfully. He was a plump man of about fifty-five who looked like a schoolmaster or a civil servant. "Is that so, Inspector?"

"Not according to my information, sir."

"It doesn't sound very satisfactory."

The inspector held his peace but his expression said only too clearly, "So what?"

"All I did last night was help a young lady who was in danger of being seriously hurt," I said. "I would like to know whether the police are calling her as a witness."

The magistrate looked at the inspector. "Are you?"

"Not at this stage, sir."

The magistrate frowned. Then, turning to me, he enquired, "What is your occupation?"

I told him. He looked surprised.

"I will adjourn this case for seven days," he announced. "That will give you time to consult a solicitor." He turned to the inspector. "Have the police any objections to bail?"

"Yes, sir."

"On what grounds?"

"We are concerned that witnesses might be intimidated, sir. Also, there is a possibility of more serious charges at a later stage."

You bastard! I thought. I was almost overwhelmed by a feeling of helplessness. The Establishment machine was grinding inexorably to ensure I was kept out of the way and there was nothing I could do about it.

For several seconds the inspector and the magistrate stared at each other. I wondered if I was allowing hope to prevail over my judgement. I was pretty sure they cordially disliked each other. Perhaps the older man regarded the younger as over-zealous. Or the policeman considered the magistrate given to deliberately making life difficult for the police, siding with defendants and caring too much about the rights of people who were patently guilty.

"The defendant has a steady, responsible job," the magistrate observed. "You wouldn't describe him as a drifter, with no fixed abode, would you, Inspector?"

"No, sir."

"Or likely to abscond?"

This time the inspector said nothing. He was probably wondering what his superiors and Roberts were going to say.

"Bail granted in the sum of fifty pounds in his own recognizances," the magistrate announced.

The inspector seemed unperturbed. I supposed he considered he had done what he had been instructed to do and it wasn't his fault if he had been overruled. You won some and you lost some. It was even possible he hadn't liked his brief.

The formalities completed, I was free to go. Outside it was as hot as ever. The air might smell of exhaust fumes, but after the stench of the cells it seemed fresh and lovely. I crossed the paved area in front of the court building and turned right along the Ridings. Nobody stared at me, nobody was interested. I was as anonymous as the first morning I came to Lemsfield, and the longer it stayed that way the better.

The old man selling papers outside the betting shop was wearing an overcoat in spite of the heat. I bought a *Standard*

and glanced at the front page. The headline read, "NATO
BREAK-UP NEAR?"

The bank was closed, and as I rang the bell the apprehension I had felt earlier returned. Nobody had been in court, but
that didn't mean they hadn't heard. But Bill Old greeted me
with no more than his habitual gloom, and the cashiers' expressions exhibited only casual interest. My apprehension began to fade.

Caroline was coming out of her room. As she turned to see
who was behind her, I saw the uncertainty in her eyes, and for
a moment I thought she was going to say something about the
previous evening. If so, she changed her mind, for she walked
off with no more than a quick smile. Did she know? I wondered. Had she known all along, been responsible for Roberts'
knowing where to find me? No, that was impossible; there was
no way she could have foreseen the fighting and that I would
take her home.

Trevor was in the staff-room compiling comparative statistics for the report. He looked up when I walked in, his expression only mildly curious; it was normal practice for me to let
him or Ben know if I wouldn't be in the next morning and I
hadn't done so. At least it meant nobody had told him.

"I'll explain later," I promised. "Where's Ben?"

"Interviewing staff. He's in the waiting-room."

That reminded me I still had people to see myself, Caroline
and Waites among them. The temptation to postpone Caroline's interview as long as possible was still there.

"Has anybody told district office I haven't been here today?" I asked.

Trevor shook his head. "No."

That was something. I considered whether to tell them
myself or wait until they saw the papers and rang me; they
had copies of all the local rags sent to them. Better get in first,
I decided.

"How's it going?" I enquired.

"All right."

We talked about routine matters for a few minutes, then I went downstairs. A pretty dark girl of seventeen or eighteen was coming out of the waiting-room. She slid past me and tripped off along the corridor, high heels tapping, buttocks swaying in her tight skirt. Ben whistled not quite silently and grinned.

"Have you finished in here?" I asked him.

"Just about. Do you want it?"

"If you don't."

"No, that's okay. We thought you weren't coming in."

"I had to go somewhere," I said, answering the implied question.

When Ben had collected his papers and departed, I closed the door and sat down at the desk. The chair was still warm from his occupancy. I thought for a minute or two; then, reluctantly, picked up the phone and asked Cathy Pallett to get me Mr. Anniss at district office.

At first he wouldn't believe me. When he did he was shocked, but in the end he agreed to postpone telling the Chief until he read about it in the papers. That meant it would be Friday at the earliest before the Old Man received his memo. It wasn't long, but it was the best I could hope for, and Anniss wouldn't relish the prospect of the Chief's breathing fire and brimstone all over him; there were a lot of people whose awe of George Hudson amounted almost to fear—including, rumour had it, several of the board.

"It was all a mistake," I said, wishing it had been.

When I had put the phone down, I went along to Caroline's room. She was signing her post, and when I asked if she could spare me a minute she looked as if she would like to say no.

"If it's about last night, I'm sorry," she said, avoiding my eye.

"What for? Calling me a paranoiac with an overheated imagination or kissing me?"

She blushed delightfully. "Both, I suppose."

"I'll forgive you for the first."

"And the second?"

"That too—only, you don't have to apologize for it. I thought perhaps you meant what happened after I left you."

"After? What did happen?"

"Haven't you heard? There were two policemen waiting for me when I got out of the lift. I spent last night and most of today in the cells. Then they took me into court and tried to get me remanded in custody, only the magistrate wasn't having any."

"What for?" Caroline was frowning.

"Assault and a breach of the peace. They said there might be more serious charges later."

"I don't understand."

"Guess."

"I can't."

"They wanted me out of the way."

"It's no good; you're talking in riddles."

"Think about it. They've only adjourned the case for a week. I'll see a solicitor and have you called as a witness."

I left her looking unhappy—she was probably afraid that she couldn't help me without damaging Sapsed's interests—and returned to the waiting-room.

Soon afterwards we left. My car was still in the car-park at the Lamb—at least I hoped it was—and I begged a lift from Trevor, who could drive home by way of the Old Town almost as easily as he could by the main road.

The TR7 was where I had left it. As far as I could tell, nobody had laid a finger on it, but there was no way I could be sure without raising the bonnet, and the yard was overlooked on three sides. I took a map from the shelf as if fetching it had been my only reason for going to the car and turned away. Was it my imagination or had the curtain at a second-floor window moved slightly?

Vickie was behind the reception desk. From the way she said, "Hallo," as bright and friendly as usual, I deduced she either hadn't read the *Star* yet or there was nothing in it about my appearance in court. I hoped it was the latter.

"I had to go away last night," I explained, picking up a copy and paying her for it. "Has anybody else come?"

By this time I had been there long enough for her not to be surprised by the question; it was like a member of a club returning after a long absence and enquiring whether any new members have joined.

"Only one: Mrs. Burrows." Vickie handed me my key.

"Is Mr. Roberts still here?"

"No, he left this morning."

Because now I knew who and what he was. And a woman had come. To take his place and keep me under observation?

"Was that her I saw in the car-park just now?" I asked Vickie. "A plump woman, about sixty?"

Vickie laughed. "No. Mrs. Burrows is about thirty-five and she isn't plump. Well, not really. I think she's still upstairs; she only got here about twenty minutes ago."

Which meant there would have been time for the police to report my release on bail and her to be instructed to come here, provided it wasn't from too far. And London wasn't too far. Either they regarded me as more naïve than I was or they didn't care. I found the second possibility the more disturbing.

There was no sign of anyone having been in my room, but it would have taken more than that to convince me. I took off my jacket and tossed it on to the bed. I felt unclean. Not just hot and grubby but dirty in a way I had never felt before, as if the taint of the cells had permeated my whole body. Taking clean clothes with me, I went along to the bathroom and turned the hot tap on full.

While I waited for the bath to fill, I glanced through the local paper. A good deal of the front page was taken up with pictures and a report of last night's scuffles, but tucked away at the bottom of a column there was a brief statement that a man had been charged with assault as a result of the incident and would appear in court today. Only me. The police must have stopped the fighting and dispersed the crowd without arresting anybody. Perhaps they had been told to calm the atmosphere as far as they could. I was the only one they wanted. No doubt the later editions would carry reports of the hearing and give my name.

After I had soaked in the bath for twenty minutes and changed into clean clothes, I felt much better and ready for a drink and a good dinner. But I couldn't linger too long over it. I had a lot to do that evening.

There were no telephones in the Lamb's bedrooms, and I stopped at the box on my way to the bar to phone Laura. She didn't answer at once, and as the bell droned monotonously I wondered if she was out. Then, rather breathlessly, she said, "Hallo?"

"Hallo. It's me," I told her ungrammatically.

"Oh hallo, darling. I half-thought you might ring last night."

"I couldn't."

"What do you mean?"

I wished I had expressed it some other way. We didn't have many secrets from each other—at least, there weren't many things I kept from Laura and I was pretty sure it was the same with her—but over the telephone was no way to explain I had spent last night in a cell and was still only free on bail.

"I'll tell you when I see you," I said. "How's your mother?" I was slightly ashamed that even now I couldn't quite bring myself to call her just "mother."

"About the same. The doctors seem quite pleased, but I—I don't know." She paused. "We've been burgled, David. At least, somebody broke into the house while Dad and I were at the hospital this afternoon. The funny thing is, they didn't take anything."

It was as though small insects were crawling all over me. Nerves, I supposed. When Roberts couldn't find the envelopes here or at our house he must have concluded I had taken them with me at the weekend and left them with Laura. He couldn't have known it wasn't until I got back I realized their importance.

"Did you call the police?" I asked.

"Yes."

"What did they say?"

"Nothing much. They seemed as if they couldn't care less. Dad was furious."

"Don't worry about it," I told her. "Whoever it was didn't get away with anything."

"I'm not worried, I just can't understand it. And I'm mad, too."

We talked for a few more minutes, then said goodbye and I went on to the bar. Mrs. Burrows came in a few minutes later. She was fairly tall and although not exactly slim, she wasn't plump, either. Her features were not bad, but she was pleasant-looking, rather than pretty, and quietly dressed. The sort of woman you would hardly notice in a crowd. I watched her surreptitiously. There was nothing indecisive about her, and she seemed completely in control of herself. If I had been asked and hadn't known better, I would have said she was a very competent teacher or a member of the junior management of some large organization.

I finished my half of bitter and went into the dining-room. The waitress came and I ordered whitebait and a steak with a salad. It was several minutes and the whitebait had come before Mrs. Burrows came in and seated herself at a table some distance from mine.

After dinner I went up to my room. Five minutes later, when I came down again, the lounge door was open and I caught a glimpse of Mrs. Burrows in a chair with her back to it. Facing her over the fireplace was a large, ornately framed mirror.

I went out to my car and sat there without switching on the ignition. Nobody else came out, and after several minutes I turned the key and drove out into the street.

FOURTEEN

There were several turnings off the dual carriageway leading up the hill to the motorway. The first led only to a small industrial estate and a dairy, and I drove past it. Approaching the second, I glanced in my mirror; none of the cars behind was within fifty yards. I flashed the left-hand indicator and turned into a quiet residential road lined with trees. Two hundred yards along, the houses gave way to a school, a low modern building standing well back from the road, behind playing-fields. I reversed into the gateway and stopped.

In the next seven minutes, while I half-listened to three records on the Triumph's radio, the only sign of life along that road was a boy of eleven or twelve riding a bike and whistling. When he had gone, I got out, lifted the TR7's bonnet and felt under the washer-bottle. The left-luggage receipt was still there, where I had concealed it yesterday, held securely to the bottom of the plastic bottle by criss-cross bands of adhesive tape. Feeling the thin paper smooth under my fingers, I realized how tense I had been. Roberts had had me arrested to give him time for a thorough search for the envelopes. He was a professional; he would hardly have overlooked my car. Last night and today, sitting in the cells at the police station and the court I had dreaded this moment, feeling for the slip of paper and finding it gone. Only when the inspector opposed bail did I dare to hope they hadn't found it yet—and even then I was afraid that wasn't the reason or that they had found it too late to tell him. Relieved, I slid into the driving-seat again.

I liked driving, the evening was fine and warm and there was little traffic on the M1; my spirits should have been high, but my enjoyment was marred by a sense of urgency, the feeling that I was fighting against time with all too little on my side.

Leaving the motorway at Junction 10, I drove down the hill, then up the other side of the valley past the airport. A big jet was taking off. The crescendo of its engines tore the evening to shreds as it climbed away to the south, making for Spain or the Mediterranean, I supposed, crowded with happy families looking forward eagerly to their holidays, blissfully ignorant of what was done in their names. Probably they wouldn't have cared if they had known.

For perhaps five seconds I wished I were with them, flying off into the blue. Escaping. Free of cares. Just free.

But I was free, I reminded myself. Free to involve myself in what I liked. To run the risk of losing my job and going to gaol.

It seemed to me as I drove down the familiar road that our house stared back at me blank and unwelcoming. Usually when I returned to it Laura was there giving it light and warmth; this evening it was empty, dead. I turned on to the drive and switched off the ignition. At least there was no dark Capri outside the Fergusons' tonight.

Next door, the garage doors were open—Nigel and Diane were out. I walked across to the front door, unlocked it and pushed it open. I didn't need to step inside to know they had been back: the state of the hall told me. It should have warned me so that I would be prepared when I went into the dining-room, but I wasn't; I stood in the doorway and stared, hardly able to believe it. This time they hadn't bothered to conceal the evidence of their being here. The room was a shambles. Drawers had been pulled out and their contents heaped anyhow on the floor.

The drawing-room was worse. The coverings on the settee and easy-chairs had been ripped and pulled back, the cushions treated in the same way. Even the carpet had been pulled up. Sick and angry, I went upstairs to our bedroom. The destruction there was much the same, it just looked worse, because the pillows had been ripped open and there were feathers everywhere. A small cloud of them wafted in the draught as I opened the door.

I felt like going down to the police station and howling abuse, but I knew it wasn't the police, not the local people, anyhow; the men who had done this were answerable only to much higher authority, and going to the police station would achieve nothing. I was thankful Laura wasn't with me; I would have time to clear up the worst of the mess and break the news more gently before she saw it.

My camera was in a heap of things they had taken from one of the cupboards in our bedroom. As I picked it up, the back flapped open; there was a film still in it. Mildly surprised they hadn't taken that to see if it contained anything useful or incriminating, I wound it on five frames for safety, found the flash-unit and for the next ten minutes photographed the main rooms in the house from a variety of angles. The police might not want to do anything, but the insurance company could hardly argue with photographic evidence.

I had taken the sixteenth shot and was about to put the camera away when the doorbell rang. I went to answer it and found Nigel and Diane in the porch.

"Come in," I told them. I wanted them to see the state of the house even if it meant their asking questions I couldn't answer.

"We saw your car outside," Diane explained. "We'd been round to Nigel's mother. How's Mrs. Stearn?"

"About the same. Laura says the doctors seem to be pleased with her." I opened the drawing-room wide. "Go in."

Diane walked as far as the threshold and stopped dead. "Oh, God!" she breathed.

Nigel looked past her and swore.

"Who did it?" Diane demanded. "Have you any idea?"

"The same people Nigel interrupted the other day, I suppose."

"Have you been to the police?"

"No. I only got here a quarter of an hour ago."

"They'll have to do something this time." Diane sounded more confident about that than I was. But then, she didn't know what I did.

"Did they come back to take your statements?" I asked.

"Yes," Nigel replied. "It was the younger one who was here Sunday night. Didn't they come to you?"

"No."

"Seems a bit odd; it's your house."

"You'll call them now, won't you, David?" Diane asked.

Any normal person would have rung them before this, I thought. I hadn't because I knew it would be pointless.

"They won't be able to do anything," I told her.

"At least they can try this time," Nigel said. "If you don't report it, you may have trouble with the insurance company."

"They may think I did it myself, you mean? Sort of arson?"

"Well, you know how difficult they can be."

"Nigel's never forgiven them for making such a fuss when he claimed for those things he burnt by mistake," Diane explained. "He thinks all insurance companies are crooked."

"All right," I agreed. "I'll call them." Why not? It would be interesting to see what line they took this time.

I rang the police station and reported what I had found, while Diane and Nigel waited, looking interested. The police promised to send somebody round right away.

"We'll get out of your hair," Nigel said. "If you give us a shout when they've gone, we'll come round and give you a hand to put things straight."

"Of course we will," Diane agreed.

"Thanks," I said, meaning it.

Suddenly she kissed me lightly on the cheek. It was the first time she had ever done that and, idiotically, I was touched. It was my week for having women kiss me unexpectedly, I thought, but her kiss didn't affect me in the way Caroline's had done.

"Poor David, you are having a time of it, aren't you?" she said.

I told myself she didn't know half of it, and I wondered what she and Nigel would say if I told them where I had spent last night and most of today.

"I'll survive," I promised. It was only after the words were out I reflected that even that was less certain than it had seemed ten days ago.

It was after ten by the time I reached the minor road just north of Lemsfield, turned right and, half a mile along it, came to a sign pointing down a still narrower lane which read, "HENSBOURN GREEN 1½."

Blackwells Farm was along a rough track. The house was grey brick, early Victorian and rectangular. Nicely proportioned, without affectation but showing distinct signs of neglect; the paintwork looked as if it hadn't been touched for a dozen years. The farm buildings were behind the house and to the right of it. One of them was collapsing into the yard, and they all needed re-roofing and a good deal more. I stopped the TR7, got out and rang the old-fashioned bell.

Nothing happened for a good twenty seconds and I was about to give the bell another chance when the door opened and I found myself face to face with Hillyer.

"I know you," he said. He frowned, as if not recognizing me worried him, but I caught the smell of whisky on his breath and reckoned it was more likely that he was having trouble focusing eyes and mind.

"We've met at the Lamb," I told him. "I'm staying there."

" 'Course. Come in."

I followed him across a hall furnished with a heavy old chest and a dresser that looked like left-overs from a previous owner which had taken root and into a big, high-ceilinged room at the back of the house. The furniture here looked as if it had been picked up cheaply at bad sales with no object but to fill up the space, and the room so lacked character I was reminded of a dingy hotel where Carole and I had stayed soon after we were married. Things hadn't started to go wrong then and we had laughed about the place afterwards. Untidily folded papers and magazines were scattered about, and ash-trays overflowed on to the two tables. A half-empty bottle of scotch stood beside a tumbler on one of the tables; the tumbler still contained a half-inch of amber-coloured liquid.

"Have a drink," Hillyer suggested amiably.

I didn't want one but decided it might be politic to accept. It wasn't hard to see why women were attracted to him: his rather arrogant good looks might be fading a bit and his drinking beginning to leave its marks, but, on the surface, at least, he still possessed an easy, self-indulgent charm. I suspected it didn't go very deep.

"Scotch?" he enquired.

"Fine," I agreed.

He fetched another glass from a cupboard and poured a good three inches of whisky into it, then as much into the glass on the table. "Water?"

"Thanks."

He had to go out to the kitchen for it; apparently he was drinking his scotch neat. When he returned he was carrying a

small china milk-jug decorated with blue flowers. It was probably the first jug he could find.

"Better do your own," he said, handing it to me. His
speech was slightly slurred. "Do I know your name?"

"It's David Grierson," I told him.

"Peter Hillyer."

"Yes, I know. You were a friend of Mrs. Sapsed's, weren't
you?"

"Who says so?" His good humour seemed suddenly to have
evaporated.

"I don't remember, somebody mentioned it. Why?"

"I knew her." The admission came grudgingly.

"It was a terrible business, her being killed like that," I said.
"It must have been a shock for you."

"Why me?"

"If she was a friend of yours."

Hillyer drank deeply and stared at me. It wasn't a friendly
look. "What the hell have you come for?" he demanded.

"I wanted to ask you something."

"What about?"

I reckoned that if it came to a fight he was the bigger and
heavier but I was probably fitter and my wind better. All the
same, I hoped it wouldn't.

"She was using you," I said. "Did you know that?"

"What d'you mean?"

"She was blackmailing Sapsed." I was watching him
closely, ready to take evasive action as soon as he started to
move. "You knew that. Whenever she wanted to screw another few hundred pounds out of him she got you to ring him
and tell him how much to leave and where. She paid you a
third for your trouble."

Blood was staining his skin under the tan. I hoped devoutly
I was right; all I had to go on were Rosemary Sapsed's will and
Sapsed's drawing too much cash and Hillyer's too little. And

Caroline's certainty that it was always a man who phoned Sapsed. It wasn't much on which to base so serious an allegation. Practically nothing.

"You bloody bastard!" he said loudly, starting forward in his chair but staying in it.

"All right," I agreed calmly. I was surprised how cool I felt now. "But you don't deny it, do you?"

"You think I'm going to waste my time denying lies like that?"

"What was she blackmailing him about?"

Hillyer stared at me. "Get out!" he blustered.

"For God's sake, don't behave like a man in a fifth-rate film," I told him.

"I'll call the police."

"Go ahead, they'll be interested." Like hell they would, I thought. They would probably run me in.

But it made him hesitate. He wasn't so drunk he didn't care about consequences. "What d'you mean?"

"They don't like blackmailers. Nor murderers."

It took a second or two for the meaning to sink in. I watched it happen and wondered if he had seriously considered the possibility that he might be suspected until now.

"I didn't kill her," he muttered.

"Didn't you?"

"Why should I?"

"Maybe you thought she'd left you something in her will."

"I wouldn't have killed her. Not Rosemary. I loved her." He was maudlin enough by now to believe it himself.

"For Christ's sake," I said disgustedly.

"I did. I liked her."

"You liked having her, you mean. It made you feel you weren't such a failure, didn't it? Having a Cabinet Minister's wife wanting to get into bed with you." All right, I was behaving like a bastard, but he deserved it; he had helped Rosemary blackmail her husband. There was something else: if it hadn't been for them my home wouldn't have been torn apart and I wouldn't have spent last night in a cell.

Even if he hadn't known about her will, he could still have killed her—because they had quarrelled or she had taunted him. Or for any of the hundred and one things which can send a man with a streak of violence too near the surface over the edge.

"Tell me what you were blackmailing him about and I'll go," I promised.

For a moment there was no answer. Hillyer was slumped in his chair. Then he said, "He had a woman somewhere."

"She told you that?"

"No, I worked it out for myself."

I had hardly touched my drink. Leaving the glass on the table, I walked to the door.

"Where were you when she was killed?" I asked, my hand on the doorknob.

"Mind your own bloody business," he muttered. He stared at me out of eyes which didn't seem to focus too well, and the last dregs of belligerence drained out of him. "I was with a girl at Luton."

The police would have checked that; they must have been satisfied. I wondered what they would have done if they found it was a lie; they wouldn't have wanted the whole sordid story coming out in court.

Leaving him in his chair, I crossed the hall and went out, closing the front door behind me.

FIFTEEN

By now it was almost dark. Some cloud had blown up during the evening and the trees were no more than silhouettes against the sky. I felt the touch of the breeze gently cool on my face, but it didn't refresh me; suddenly I was tired. So tired that all I wanted was to drive back to the Lamb and sleep. I knew the tiredness wasn't purely physical, that in part it was the reaction after the events of the last few days, but that did nothing to alleviate my annoyance; I was young and prided myself on my fitness. I resented being so weary when I had hardly exerted myself physically for days. But what happened to me no longer seemed to be happening to someone else. Even that small measure of relief was denied me now.

I reached my car, got in and started the engine. Ten minutes, I promised myself. Perhaps less. Then all I had to do was walk up the stairs, open the door of my room and fall into bed.

Along the narrow lane I saw no other car, not even a light from any house, but ahead the sky was bright, the clouds reflecting the lights of Lemsfield. The Old Town was almost deserted. I turned in under the arch and felt the cobbles jar the TR7's suspension. The single lamp which more or less illuminated the car-park was out. At first I couldn't see a space and I had to drive right to the end before I found one, between a Rover 2600 and a Capri. I manoeuvred into it, switched off the Triumph's ignition, then the lights, and slid out.

It was dark here by the wall and I saw nothing. Heard no sound. One moment the air was fresh, the next an arm was wrapped tight round me from behind and something was pressing against my face. Something soft that smelt sweet and cloying.

Almost instinctively I fought against the nauseating pressure. My assailant's left arm was pinioning mine while he held the pad of cloth or whatever it was over my face with his right, but in the darkness he couldn't see me clearly and he hadn't judged it quite right: the pad was pressing against my cheek, rather than my nose and mouth. Nevertheless my head was swimming and I knew that if I inhaled much more of the sickening fumes I would pass out cold. I drove my right elbow back as hard as I could in the limited space and wrenched my body to the left.

My attacker must have been taken by surprise, I felt him stagger, off balance, and the pressure on my face slackened. But I had breathed in enough of the chloroform or whatever it was to make me muzzy. Opening my mouth, I gulped in fresh air. It helped a little, but the next second he flung himself on me and I staggered back against the Triumph. Its hood was down and the jarring impact sent me half falling into the car. He followed up his advantage immediately, giving me no time to regain my balance.

By now my eyes were becoming accustomed to the near-darkness, and as he came at me I saw it was Roberts. From somewhere I summoned up enough strength to push him away, but the respite was short-lived, he came forward again, driving his right knee hard into the pit of my stomach. This time my gasp was involuntary. I felt the wind whistle out of my lungs agonizingly, and as I doubled up, gasping for breath, he pressed the pad over my nose and mouth. My head swam, I felt the strength going out of my limbs, and the next second everything went blank.

When I came to, it was no longer dark. A strange silvery light bathed everything, and I was cold. A damp chill seemed to have seeped right into my bones. Then I realized that the silvery light was the moon and I was lying on damp grass. Either it had rained or there had been a heavy dew. There was no grass in the car-park; Roberts must have moved me so that I wouldn't be found when people came out to their cars. I felt sick and my head ached. I wondered how long I had been out and tried to sit up. It was a mistake; moving made the nausea worse and my head ache more violently.

Standing would be worse still, I told myself, but I couldn't stay here all night. Already my shirt and trousers were wet. By working my way laboriously on to my hands and knees, then pulling myself up by the back of a garden bench, I made it. I had been right; it was worse. Much worse. And being proved right was small consolation. I stood there, clinging to the bench, hoping the sharp throbbing in my head and the longing to be sick would pass.

They didn't altogether, but after a few minutes they became more muted and I was able to think about other things. I was in the small garden behind the hotel, on the other side of a brick wall from the car-park. My feet were damp, but it was a few seconds before I realized I wasn't wearing any shoes. The grass felt damp and rough through my thin socks. My jacket had gone too, and there was a soreness in my left arm. I had experienced the same feeling often enough before to know what it was: somebody had stuck a hypodermic needle in me. That explained why I had been out so long, chloroform alone would have worked for only a quarter of an hour or so once the pad was removed from my nose and mouth. Roberts had come prepared.

My shirt was pulled out of my trousers. I supposed that had happened while we were struggling, but when I tried to put my hand in my pocket for my handkerchief, I couldn't; all my pockets had been turned inside out. I wondered dully where my keys were. But first I wanted my shoes. I felt oddly vulnerable without them.

It didn't take me long to find them; they were only a few feet from where I was standing, but when I picked them up there seemed to be something strange about them. Then I saw what it was: the inner soles had been torn out. Stooping to pull them on brought back the nausea, but I managed it and went down on all fours to search for the things from my pockets. They were in a little heap near where I had found my shoes.

There should be a torch in the glove compartment of the TR7. I went to find it, walking slowly, like an old man, dragging one foot after the other. My jacket was still on the passenger seat, but it wasn't folded any longer, and when I picked it up I swore impotently. The lining had been ripped out and my wallet was no longer in the breast pocket. Then I saw it on the seat. At least, I thought, I knew why Roberts had been lying in wait for me: having searched the house and my room at the Lamb, he must have concluded I was carrying the envelopes around with me. Or, if not the envelopes themselves, at least a clue to their whereabouts.

From the appearance of the interior of the car, he had given that a pretty thorough going over too. The bonnet was closed and I dared not raise it to see if the ticket was safe, in case he was still hanging about not far away, watching me. Or Mrs. Burrows; her room probably overlooked the car-park.

I looked over at the side wall of the hotel. It was in darkness. Until now I had been too busy with other things and too muzzy to take that in or to consider the implications. Now I did. The Lamb had no night porter and I didn't fancy spending the rest of the night in my car.

I started walking towards the street. It called for a ridiculous effort to cover more than a few yards, but I persevered and Fate must have decided she had played enough dirty tricks on me lately; there was a light in a window just before the arch leading to the street. From what I knew of the layout of the place, I reckoned it was the manager's office. I tapped on the glass, praying the light hadn't been left on inadvertently and everybody wasn't in bed.

After a few seconds one of the curtains was pulled aside. The figure was only a silhouette against the light, but beyond it I could see three men sitting round a table playing cards. There were glasses and two bottles on the table. I knew none of them and assumed it was Deards, the manager, who had come to the window. He must have recognized me, for he nodded and gestured towards the front door.

By the time I got there he had it open.

"Sorry," I apologized, "I got held up."

He gave me a quizzical look, it was very late and I must have looked a mess. "You're lucky it's Wednesday," he observed, "it's my night for doing the books."

"Yes," I agreed.

He grinned. He was in his mid-thirties, a burly man with fair hair and a pleasant manner. Usually he wore a dark suit, but now he was in his shirt-sleeves. "Goodnight," he said.

I was half-way up the first flight of stairs when he called quietly. "Oh, Mr. Grierson, I heard Mrs. Burrows asking Vickie if she knew whether you'd gone out this evening and when you were likely to get back. I think she'd found something of yours."

For several seconds my heart seemed to stop beating. Then I told myself it couldn't be the ticket; she wouldn't have mentioned that if she had found it and, anyway, it had still been safe under the bonnet of my car after I left the Lamb about seven forty-five. She must have wanted to know when I was likely to return, in order to tell Roberts.

"I expect I'll see her in the morning," I said. "Thanks. Goodnight."

I went up to my room, let myself in and stretched out on the bed without undressing. I felt terrible. If Roberts and his masters wanted the envelopes so badly he was ready to go to these lengths to get them, why not let him have them? He was a professional; what hope had I against him and all he represented? Should I even try to stand in his way?

The temptation went as quickly as it had come. If I handed the envelopes over, they would be destroyed and the whole business would be hushed up. Sapsed would get away with murder. Literally.

It was no good my going to the police, they had already made that abundantly clear. I was on my own.

Once again I tried to make some sort of sense of what I knew. Both Caroline and Hillyer had maintained Mrs. Sapsed had been blackmailing her husband because she had discovered his affair with Caroline. True, Hillyer hadn't known it was Caroline, but that made no difference. Were they right? Would Sapsed really have been so afraid of the affair becoming public knowledge?

But if not, what had it been about?

I tried to force my fuddled brain to concentrate, but it was no use. Every time, I got so far and came up against a blank wall. In the end, I gave up, undressed and climbed into bed. My last waking thought was of Laura.

My alarm-clock woke me. I rolled over to turn it off and wondered why my head throbbed painfully and there was a foul taste in my mouth. Then I remembered.

By the time I had washed, shaved and cleaned my teeth I felt slightly more human. I took a couple of aspirins and went downstairs.

Mrs. Burrows entered the dining-room just after me, and as

she passed my table she gave me the polite half-smile fellow-residents in hotels exchange when they recognize each other but haven't got round to speaking. It was so ordinary a gesture and seemed so spontaneous I might have asked myself whether, after all, I might be wrong about her if it hadn't been for what Deards had told me last night. If she had found something of mine, why hadn't she stopped to tell me so instead of walking past?

I ordered orange juice, toast and coffee and opened my *Telegraph*. The NATO crisis was worsening and the defence ministers of the allied powers were meeting in London on Saturday and Sunday in an attempt to resolve it. I stared at the page as if hypnotized.

"Excuse me, sir." The elderly waitress was trying to put down the plate on which was poised my glass of orange juice.

I apologized and moved the paper out of her way. Was that the real explanation of all that had happened to me? Not merely that Sapsed wanted the envelopes back, but that the people who possessed the real power, above even the rank and file in the Cabinet, didn't care whether he had murdered his wife. All that mattered was that no breath of scandal must touch him until the crisis was resolved one way or the other. Why not? More extraordinary things happened every day; the incredible had become almost routine. And it had a terrible logic.

Was that why the police had taken in Garvie for questioning? Not because they thought he had been involved in Mrs. Sapsed's death, but to distract attention from her husband? To the powers-that-be it would have seemed simple; nothing must be seen or done which would undermine in the slightest Sapsed's standing at the present time. It would take very little to persuade the Americans to withdraw from the alliance, and there was no time to replace him before the meeting at the weekend.

Oh, God! I thought.

The waitress returned, removed my empty glass and brought a rack of toast.

This business was far bigger, far more dangerous than I had believed. The police would release Garvie—perhaps they had done so already—and gradually the public would lose interest in the case. In a week or two it would be virtually forgotten except by a circle of his friends and some local people.

In the meantime, if Roberts and Mrs. Burrows couldn't find the envelopes, what would they do? I preferred not to think about that.

Mrs. Burrows was still at her table, drinking a second cup of coffee and reading her paper, when I finished my breakfast. I toyed with the idea of going across and asking her what it was of mine she had found, but she would only express surprise and say there must have been some mistake; she hadn't found anything.

I went up to my room for my brief-case. When I came down again, she had gone and a waitress was clearing her table.

SIXTEEN

Just before eleven, I walked round to the post office and rang Catlow's paper.

"I thought you were going to call yesterday," he said.

"I couldn't."

Maybe it was something in my tone made him ask, "What happened?"

"I was arrested Tuesday evening. They kept me locked up until yesterday afternoon."

"*You?* Christ. What had you done? Rape?"

I imagined him grinning; it would be the hell of a joke to Catlow.

"According to them, assault and conduct likely to cause a breach of the peace."

"Had you?"

"No. There was a demo because the police had taken a student in for questioning. It turned into a punch-up and I went to help a girl who'd been knocked over."

"Young Sir Galahad," Catlow commented, still amused.

"It's not funny being locked up in a cell and having the police opposing bail," I told him warmly. "It was a frame-up; they wanted me out of the way."

"Why?"

"I'll tell you later."

"Was it something to do with the other business?"

"It looks like it."

"There could be a story there."

"Get stuffed," I said rudely. "Did you find out anything?"

"Not a lot. The lady's first husband committed suicide."

I hadn't known that; not surprisingly, it hadn't been in her obituary. "Do you know why?" I asked.

"No. But it seems there were some rather nasty stories about her at the time."

"Other men?"

"No."

"What sort of stories, then?"

"That she was some kind of sadist. Not quite normal. Something like that anyway. None of it came out at the inquest. Her second husband divorced her after a year."

"They don't do the gentlemanly thing any more," I commented.

"It would probably be an offence: sexual discrimination."

"What was Sapsed doing between the time he left Wessex University, in June '67, and taking up the job at Conservative Central Office, in '69?"

"Nothing in particular, as far as I could find out. He seems to have been abroad a good bit; he had a spell doing research in Prague."

"*Where?*"

"It's in Czechoslovakia," Catlow said. "That was in Dubček's time; things were pretty relaxed."

I wondered if Sapsed could have been working for our intelligence people there. On the other hand—

"Is he a queer?" I asked. If he was, not only might it explain why his marriage had gone wrong—although his wife's history was sufficient explanation of that—it might explain a good deal more besides. Then I remembered Caroline. "Bisexual, then?"

"No," Catlow answered. He sounded positive about it.

"You're sure?"

"Pretty sure. Parliament's a close little world, you know,

members, correspondents and the rest. Things like that get known. Just because there's no public scandal it doesn't mean people there don't know."

"No," I agreed. So what had Rosemary known about Sapsed? Whatever it was, he had kept it from Caroline and let her think he was being blackmailed about their affair. "What do they think of him?" I enquired.

"According to our parliamentary people, he's well liked. Good at his job and respected by the other side."

"Did you find out what time he got to the House that night?"

"He was in the Chamber at ten-thirty; he spoke in the defence debate later. I couldn't find anyone who knew what time he arrived at the House without people asking questions. I didn't think you'd want that."

"No," I agreed.

"Does it help?"

"I'm not sure."

"You don't seriously think he did it, do you?"

I could hear the scepticism in Catlow's voice. "I don't know," I told him.

"David." He paused. "Look, if I were you I'd keep out of it. Don't get involved."

"Do you know something?" I demanded.

"No, it's just a feeling. The water could be pretty rough. And murky."

He could say that again. All the same, I wondered if he had been wholly frank when he said he didn't know anything. Not that it made any difference.

"I am involved," I told him. "But I'll be careful. Thanks, Jack."

"I'm beginning to understand why they wanted you out of the way," he said.

"That's right." I laughed. I had no intention of telling him about the envelopes.

Outside, in the street, people were going about their lives neither knowing nor caring who had killed Rosemary Sapsed. Her death hadn't been even a nine-day wonder; today was only the eighth since she was murdered and already, even here in Lemsfield, it was half-forgotten. Why was I bothering?

Because I knew, I told myself.

How much I knew and how much that I suspected was the truth didn't matter, I knew too much to turn my back and walk away pretending none of it had really happened or that it was nothing to do with me.

Sapsed. Hillyer. Carthy. Perhaps Monique Chabrier. Almost certainly one of them had killed Rosemary Sapsed. True, there might be a fifth person of whom I knew nothing, but the odds were still heavily on its being one of those four. And Sapsed I could rule out; he had been with Caroline.

I walked round to the Conservative offices. The only member of the staff in evidence was a dark, plain girl who seemed to be the typist and general clerk. She told me Mr. Carthy was in and went to let him know I wanted to see him.

She left the door open a few inches and I could hear him complaining that she shouldn't have admitted he was there and he didn't want to see me. I didn't blame him; he was probably embarrassed by the memory of the other evening, when I had taken him home.

I walked through. He was sitting at a big, old-fashioned desk looking petulant and unwell.

"Hallo, Martyn," I said.

"Oh, it's you. I didn't know."

I noticed he avoided the girl's eye. She looked from him to me and back again uncertainly and went out, closing the door this time.

"Feeling better?" I asked him.

"Better?" He moved uneasily.

"Than the other evening. You weren't too well then."

"Oh. Yes thanks. Things had been a bit difficult."

"I can imagine."

I looked round. The room was small and dingy, and not much light filtered in through the window; it overlooked a tiny yard, and the outsides of the panes were filthy. Dust danced in what light there was. The only pictures were a portrait of the Queen and, in too close proximity to it to be entirely respectful, a calendar with a picture of a very naked, very nubile girl. I wondered if the disrespect was deliberate and decided it wasn't; Carthy hadn't that sort of sense of humour.

"Have the police been to see you again?" I asked him. He nodded. "Did they want to know where you were the night Mrs. Sapsed was killed?"

"Yes."

"Where were you?"

"It's none of your bloody business."

"Maybe not," I agreed. "On the other hand, it could be."

"What do you mean?"

"My house has been broken into twice and left as if a bomb had hit it, my room at the Lamb has been searched, I've been locked in a cell all night and charged with something I didn't do and last night I was drugged. My father-in-law's house has been searched and my next-door neighbour coshed. Do you still say it's nothing to do with me?" I was getting tired of cataloguing it, but I intended him to know.

"You don't think I had anything to do with any of that?" Carthy looked shaken.

"No, I'm damned sure you hadn't. I just want to get this mess cleared up and live a normal, peaceful life again. And if you think the police are going to help, you're wrong; they've been warned off. It would look bad if the Minister of Defence was charged with murdering his wife. Especially just now."

"You don't think Gerald—"

"He can't have, can he? But who else knows that?" I paused. "You went to see her that night, didn't you? What happened?"

"Nothing." He was lying and he wasn't a good liar.

For a moment neither of us spoke. The cheap clock on the mantelpiece ticked loudly.

"All right, why did you go?"

"I had to see her about something."

"And?"

"Nothing. I told you."

"Then, what did you quarrel about?" Had they quarrelled? It was clear something had happened, something Carthy didn't want to talk about.

"We didn't." Our eyes met and he looked away. A flush like a boy's stained his cheeks. "She laughed at me," he muttered. "Said I hadn't the guts to ask her to sleep with me. She said why didn't we go to bed then; Gerald wouldn't be back for hours. I didn't know what to say; I knew she was laughing at me and she didn't mean it. Then she told me to clear out and stick to the only thing I could do properly and stop playing being a man because I never would."

I asked myself why I had pressed him to tell me. I hadn't wanted to hear that; now I was sharing his humiliation.

"It wasn't just you," I said. "She was like that with a lot of people. Maybe she couldn't help it."

Whoever had killed her had done the world a good turn.

"You left then?" I asked. He nodded. "What time was that?"

"About half-past nine."

I could imagine his state then, almost desperate with bitterness and shame. He must have hated Rosemary Sapsed.

Enough to kill her? It wasn't hard to picture him standing in the wood, the bitterness fermenting inside him, waiting for her to come that way. He would have known about her taking the dogs for a walk when Sapsed was away.

And when she did? They would have known him, they wouldn't have barked.

"Where did you go when you left her?"

"Home."

"Straightaway?"

"I sat in my car for a minute or two; that's all."

"And you didn't see anyone else near the house or on the road?"

"No."

That might, just possibly, point to Monique Chabrier. On the other hand, he was probably in no condition to notice anybody who had been there.

"Thanks," I said.

"You're going now?"

"Unless there's something else you have to tell me."

He shook his head, almost reluctantly it seemed, as if he no longer wanted me to leave him. Perhaps, after all, telling me had been a relief.

In the outer office the dark girl was filing papers in a cabinet. I hoped she hadn't heard too much.

Outside in the street it was hotter than ever. Sweat showed in dark patches on men's shirts and between the shoulders of women's dresses. There was no sign of the weather breaking yet. I started to walk back along the Ridings.

After the glare in the street, inside the bank it was half dark and blessedly cool, but I knew that within a few minutes my shirt would be sticking to my back again. I sat down in the waiting-room and opened my brief-case; for the rest of the day I had better concentrate on my real job; the inspection should be completed this week and I still had to see Caroline and

Waites, finish my report and discuss it with Waites tomorrow. Ben and Trevor had already almost exhausted their programme and were wondering how much longer I meant to stay here.

I took out Caroline's report. Hell! I thought. The other evening, when I walked out of her flat, I had been running away because I knew what would happen if I didn't. I wanted it to happen. Yesterday, when she apologized, I had felt about two feet tall. Now I had to interview her. Picking up the three copies of her report, I walked along to her room and tapped on the door.

As I glanced through that evening's edition of the *Star* in the bar before dinner, an advertisement caught my eye: the Rt. Hon. Gerald Sapsed, MP, would be holding a "surgery" at the Conservative offices the following evening. He was going to have a busy weekend, unless he called off the "surgery."

When I returned to the bar, an hour later, Hillyer was there at the other end of the room talking to two men I hadn't seen before. I thought once that he had noticed me, but if he had, he was no more anxious for my company than I was for his, and he looked away again without any sign of recognition. Carthy didn't put in an appearance.

Just before nine, I went up to my room to watch the BBC news. There was a good deal about the background to the NATO ministers' meeting, but mostly it was stuff I had heard several times before. Nevertheless, it was clear the government was worried.

I waited for the weather forecast—the hot dry spell was expected to end tomorrow and there was a likelihood of thunder storms over southern England—then switched off the set. I had a lot of hard thinking to do.

SEVENTEEN

Only a few of the staff had arrived when I reached the bank the next morning. Harry Roche was there, and Caroline Bedford came in a few minutes later; Waites rarely arrived before nine fifteen.

The stationery store was a small room next to the machine-room. I found two large envelopes, one big enough to take the other unfolded, and took them back to the waiting-room. There I addressed the larger of the two to the manager at the branch at Cressford, where Laura and I kept our joint account, and slipped into it a letter I had written the previous evening. The letter was quite short, merely a request to hold the envelope which was enclosed on my behalf unopened until I claimed it and not to release it to anyone else, even if they appeared to hold my authority to withdraw it. I put both envelopes into my brief-case and locked it.

That done, I began to read the report which I had completed yesterday afternoon. There were three copies, one for the department, one for district office and one which would eventually be sent to Waites with the district manager's comments. When I had finished checking the top copy, I locked it and one of the others in my brief-case and took the third along to the manager's room.

Caroline Bedford was with him. I murmured an apology and said I would come back later, but he interrupted me grandly.

"Don't go, Mr. Grierson. We had just finished."

I looked out of the window and tried to close my ears while he resumed his conversation with Caroline. It wasn't easy to ignore his rich, rather loud tones, but I thought about Laura and what we would do if she came home that weekend.

It was several minutes before Waites finished, and Caroline flashed me the ghost of a smile as she passed me on her way out. I explained I had completed my report and would be grateful for an opportunity to go through it with him when he had read it and had a few minutes to spare. It goes against the grain with me but it's simpler and, in the end, more productive to lay on the respect with a trowel when you're dealing with a man like Waites. Stop short of creeping and you'll keep your self-respect and get what you want without his even knowing it. Some people call it diplomacy, others crawling; it depends on your point of view. I hated it but sometimes found it necessary.

"You'll be finishing today?" he asked.

"I think so."

He nodded gravely and opened his diary. From where I was standing I could see there were only two appointments for that day.

"Two-thirty?" he suggested.

"Thank you."

I left him the report and returned to the waiting-room, reflecting that for the first time for several days I had a fairly clear conscience. My report was written and typed and the inspection should be completed on time. True, I had flagrantly disobeyed the Chief's injunction to have nothing to do with the Sapsed affair, but other people had made it impossible for me to obey him.

There was a telephone directory in one of the desk drawers. I pulled it out, looked up the number of the Conservative offices and asked Cathy Pallett to give me a line. The phone buzzed in my ear. I dialled the number and got a dead line. I swore, decided I must be more on edge than I had realized and tried again. This time I was successful and after a few rings Carthy answered.

When I told him who I was he didn't sound too pleased.

"Do you know if Sapsed will be at home this evening?" I asked him.

"Why?"

"I want to see him."

"He's got a surgery here at seven; you could see him then."

"Too public," I said.

"What do you want to see him about?"

"I've got something he wants." Poor Carthy, he was worried it was something to do with him. "It's all right, it's nothing you need worry about."

"I wish I could be sure of that."

He sounded so miserable I nearly laughed. But it wasn't funny; he was probably scared stiff the police would suspect him of murdering Rosemary Sapsed because of what had happened that night. And equally scared that his humiliation would become public knowledge. He didn't see that most of the people who knew him were already aware of his infatuation and thought no worse of him because of it.

"Tell him it's something he's been asking about," I said. "Will you?"

"All right," Carthy agreed, "I'll tell him. What time will you be there?"

"About nine. Thanks, Martyn."

"I just wish I knew what was going on," he complained.

I ignored the implied question and hung up. I wasn't sure I could answer it anyway.

There was a train to London at ten thirty-four; I would catch that. But before then I must have a word with Harry Roche about a few matters which, while they weren't important enough to be included in the report, had to be mentioned. Mostly they were details of procedure and controls. I walked to the door and was surprised to find it wasn't latched; I was almost sure I had closed it properly when I came in. Looking out, I saw the twitch of a skirt rounding the corner at the end of the corridor.

Cars were entering and leaving the car-park in two endless processions, Friday-morning shoppers adding to the usual weekday traffic. I could see nobody I knew. Taking out the plastic bottle of water I always carried in case of emergencies, I opened the bonnet and topped up the washer-bottle. Nobody took any notice of me and, if they had, it was unlikely they would have seen me retrieve the left-luggage ticket before I closed the bonnet again. I slid into the driving-seat, started the engine and drove out into the street between a green MGB and a Renault 5. In the rear-view mirror I saw a grey Capri follow the Renault and my heart lurched.

I told myself not to jump to conclusions, there were thousands of Capris about, but I couldn't quite dispel a nagging fear that this one, following me across the river and turning into the Ridings behind me, was Roberts'.

The station car-park had a "Full" notice up at the entrance. I drove round a couple of corners, found a space in a back street and parked. When I walked back, the Capri was parked on a double yellow line thirty yards past the entrance to the booking-hall. The ticket seemed to be burning a hole in my pocket; the last thing I wanted was a confrontation with Roberts now.

Even on that brilliantly sunny day the booking-hall was gloomy. I bought a return to Euston and walked out through the other door to the platform. According to the digital clock, there was still thirteen minutes to go before the train was due, and for the first two or three of them I was going to have the platform to myself. Feeling lonely and exposed and keeping the brick building between me and the exit from the booking-hall, I started walking towards the unwinking red signal light at the southern end of the platform. Past the two waiting-rooms and the sign "Gentlemen" above a shabby wooden screen from behind which came the hiss of jetting water. Past two benches and a flat trolley loaded with a single mail-bag. Across the rails on the other platform there was a poster advertising a local estate agent and, sitting beneath it, a girl in jeans and a shirt. She had a mass of tightly curled fair hair and a bored expression. Seeing me looking at her, she stared back haughtily, then looked away.

By now other people were drifting on to the platform from the booking-hall. Women's heels clacked and a baby cried. There was no sign of Roberts. I felt tense, on edge. Where was he? I would rather have seen him, known he was here, than wait, wondering.

Dead on time, almost silently, the train glided in and doors opened. Alone by the first coach, I found a seat in a compartment with only two passengers, lowered the window and leaned out, watched resentfully by the middle-aged woman in the opposite seat. The passengers who had left the train were moving away towards the exit; those boarding it had already found seats. A porter looked back at the guard, then turned towards the driver. Another few seconds, I thought. Then a man came out of the booking-hall, walked quickly across the platform and swung himself up into a compartment near the back of the train. It was Roberts. Before the door closed behind him the train glided forward.

The train was scheduled to run non-stop to Euston. I considered pulling the communication cord as it passed through the suburbs and jumping out as it came to a stop, but a single figure running off would be more noticeable than one man in the throng at Euston. I would have to wait and take my chance there.

The fact that Roberts had been in the car-park must mean he had been keeping me under surveillance; had he seen me take the luggage ticket from under the bonnet of my car?

Almost the whole length of the train separated his compartment from mine, and I reckoned that gave me about seventy yards start. Say nine seconds. More important, there should be a lot of passengers getting out between us, and he was probably counting on my not having spotted him board the train.

I studied the other two people in my compartment. The girl in the window-seat diagonally across from me was about eighteen. Her hair hung lankly below her shoulders and she was wearing a cheap, crumpled dress and grubby shoes. She twitched regularly and made tiny movements with her hands as though she were moving to the rhythm of music only she could hear. Perhaps one shouldn't judge by appearances, but she didn't impress me as either reliable or intelligent. Not even very clean. The woman opposite me was a very different proposition; she had glasses, tightly waved grey hair and a severe expression. Her blouse with a brooch at the neck and skirt and shoes were eminently sensible. She looked reliable; if I explained that I needed a package-fetching from the left-luggage office at King's Cross and couldn't go myself because I had to wait for somebody, would she collect it for me? I doubted it; she looked too reliable. She might well decide the request was suspicious and go to the police. Her features, which, if severe, had seemed commonplace and pleasant enough until now, suddenly seemed to acquire a relentless probity. She looked the sort of woman who would always know what was right and do it, regardless of the consequences for other people. Anyway, it would be unreasonable to ask a stranger to go from Euston to King's Cross and back. And if I went myself and failed, at least I would have only myself to blame.

Stations flashed past, blurs of platforms, signs and fretwork buildings in the depressing suburbs. Then, almost too soon for me, the train slowed and pulled in to Euston. Before it stopped I had the door open and was running along the platform, hoping the crowd of alighting passengers would shield me from Roberts' eyes. But I knew that in another few seconds, running up the slope to the concourse, I would be as conspicuous as I would have been fleeing from the train if I had pulled the communication cord. And crossing it there would be no shelter. But I had to run, to make myself conspicuous, because if I didn't, Roberts would catch up with me before I reached the top of the slope.

I flashed my ticket at the collector and raced on. I had no idea where I was going when I reached the top: The men's lavatory had a single combined entrance and exit, the bars and buffets were glass-fronted. There was almost certain to be a queue for taxis with little hope of claiming one before Roberts appeared. Similarly, if I went down to the Underground I might have to wait minutes for a train.

Then I remembered having seen a while-you-wait photograph kiosk between the top of the slope which led down to Platform One and the toilets. It was one of those automatic affairs. I swerved to my left, glancing back over my shoulder as I did so. I couldn't be sure, but I thought I saw Roberts' tall figure pushing through the crush at the ticket barrier.

There were plenty of people moving about the concourse, but I would have liked more. There were too many open spaces. I dodged past the row of people gazing up at the big arrival and departure boards and the queue at the confectionery kiosk. Thirty yards ahead was the photograph booth.

If anyone had been using it I would have been cornered, but my luck was in. I slipped inside, sat down and drew the curtains. It was only then I realized something I had forgotten, or had never noticed before: the curtains were only half length and left me exposed from the waist down. If Roberts came this way, he could hardly miss seeing there was somebody in the booth.

But it was too late to worry about that. I had to count on his assuming I had gone straight on to the Underground or the street.

Tense, heart pounding, I stayed in my cramped quarters while the minute hand of my watch moved a sixth of the way round the dial. The ten minutes seemed more like an hour. I could hear two young male voices only a few feet away. At first it was desultory talk, then impatient, aimed at me. For all I knew, Roberts was standing just outside, waiting for me to emerge, but I could see nothing.

I came out from my cover. The boys were seventeen or eighteen, dressed in tee-shirts and jeans. And they were alone. Roberts couldn't be watching from the toilet. Men were going in and out of the door all the time, but there were too many windows, too many places in that vast concourse where he might be.

Wherever he was, I couldn't remain here. Looking left and right, I walked briskly towards the steps which led down to the Underground, fifty yards away, pushed two coins into the machine for my ticket and headed for the Victoria Line escalator, wondering whether Roberts was ahead of me or behind.

There were only a few people on the escalator, a blonde girl in a sundress, two youths, an elderly woman, two men in business suits. No Roberts. I felt the relief untying my nerves.

Then I saw him, coming towards me on the ascending escalator. He must have seen me at the same moment, he was looking straight at me, but he gave no sign and the next second he looked away. I felt as isolated as I had done on the platform at Lemsfield as slowly the gap between us narrowed. Somebody ran past, jostling me and muttering an apology.

Then, for a fraction of a second we were level. The next he had passed, borne irresistibly upward.

I ran down the last twenty-odd steps, pushing past the two boys who were standing almost abreast, half blocking the way. One of them swore at my back. At the bottom I looked over my shoulder; Roberts was still some way from the top.

I had two alternatives, to make straight for one of the platforms and trust to luck a train would come before Roberts had time to catch up with me or I could get on the up escalator behind him. That way we could go round in circles all day—or until he called the police and had me arrested on some pretext. It wasn't really a choice.

I could hear a train rumbling in a tunnel, but there was nothing to tell me which line it was on. Even if it was on this level.

The north-bound platform was nearly deserted, but the sound of the train was louder now and the next second I saw its light in the tunnel. I walked towards it, away from the entrance to the platform, putting the few people waiting between me and Roberts. Then the train rattled in and doors slid open. I boarded a coach near the back, resisting a temptation to stand by the door so that I could keep an eye out for Roberts, because I knew that if I saw him he could see me. Sinking down on a seat, I tried to make myself relax.

The doors sighed shut and I told myself he hadn't had time to reach the top of the escalator and come back down. Then the doors opened again. To allow somebody who had just run on to the platform to board the train? Why did the staff have to be so helpful?

I told myself it couldn't be him. But I didn't believe it.

There was no sign of Roberts at King's Cross, so perhaps he hadn't made it after all. I waited out of sight beyond the ticket barrier for a few minutes, but he didn't appear. I walked up the tunnel to the main-line station, across the passenger

concourse and along Platform Eight to the left-luggage counter, reclaimed my package and took it next-door, to the men's
toilet. There, in the privacy of a cubicle, I opened it, extracted
three of the envelopes, transferred them to the smaller of the
two I had brought with me, sealed it with Sellotape and
placed it in the larger one with the letter. I had already put
stamps on it. Putting the other envelopes in my breast pocket,
I found a pillar-box and posted it.

When that was done I felt better, but there was still a lot to
do. I took the Tube to Euston and caught the next train back
to Lemsfield.

Laura rang soon after I arrived back at the branch; she had
decided to come home the next day. There was nothing more
she could do to help her father and she wanted to be home
again.

Just in time, I remembered the state of the house. Nigel
and Diane had helped me put the bigger things back, but it
still looked a bit like the aftermath of a hurricane.

"Which train will you catch?" I asked. "I'll meet you at the
station."

"There's no need, I can catch a bus."

And walk in to find that shambles? Not likely. "Of course
I'll meet you," I said. I would have met her anyway; the chaos
at home merely gave me an added incentive.

"I don't know which train I'll be on," Laura objected. Why
couldn't women accept an offer gracefully, without raising all
sorts of difficulties? They did in the end. "It depends what
time I get away. I want to get Dad his lunch first."

"Ring me from King's Cross, then," I told her.

"All right."

"It'll be good to have you back."

"Will it?" she asked softly.

EIGHTEEN

The Triumph's dashboard clock said seven minutes past nine. That, I told myself, was about right; scrupulous punctuality— or, worse, my being early—might have been construed as a sign of eagerness. Even weakness. I changed down to second and turned on to the drive which led to the Sapseds' house.

Overhead the sky was still blue, but in the west the clouds were piling up in dark, angry masses. It had been hot and increasingly sultry all day; now, quite suddenly, the temperature had dropped fifteen degrees. Thunder rumbled in the distance, and once or twice I saw the flicker of lightning over the hills on the other side of the valley. A furtive little wind rustled the leaves, then died. The clouds, blotting out the sun, had brought a premature dusk, and already it was half dark.

As I changed up again to third, the palm of my hand was sticky on the knob of the gear-lever, but I knew it wasn't only the coming storm. I was on edge. It seemed unlikely Sapsed would let me drive up to his house and listen to what I had to say without taking steps to prevent me, and I would have felt easier in my mind if I had known where Roberts was, but I hadn't seen him since Euston, that morning.

Ahead, half screened by the spreading branches of the cedar, the house squatted at the end of the drive, looking far too tranquil to be the setting for violence. I stopped the car in front of it, switched off the engine and sat there, looking round, my ears strained to catch any noise. Somewhere in the wood to my left a bird called, the atmosphere making the sound seem clearer. A car hooted on the main road, but nothing moved.

I looked at the front door, fifteen yards away. What lay behind it? I had no way of telling whether Sapsed was alone, and it required more will power than I liked to slip the carkeys into my pocket and get out. Was Roberts or one of his colleagues waiting somewhere in the half-lit gloom, maybe only a few yards away, watching every step I took, a gun trained on me?

I made myself walk towards the door, my legs strangely stiff and heavy, remembering another occasion when I had felt the same sensation: approaching old Russell Sharp's house in Cressford. I thrust the memory away and rang the bell.

For perhaps a quarter of a minute there was no answer and I wondered if Sapsed wasn't there after all. Strange, it hadn't occurred to me he might choose not to keep the appointment. Then I heard footsteps in the hall. A man's steps. I watched the door opening slowly and knew it was too late to walk away.

"Good evening, Mr. Grierson," Sapsed said. "You're late."

"A few minutes," I agreed. Now I could see him I felt calmer. "I hope the tension wasn't too much for you."

For a moment he looked surprised; then he said abruptly, "You'd better come in."

I followed him into a room across the hall from that where he had seen Bates and me the other afternoon. This was a long, low, rambling sort of room with a brick fireplace and some nice old furniture. He stopped in the middle of it and faced me. I hadn't meant it when I said I hoped the tension hadn't been too much for him; I was retaliating because of his comment that I was late. And because it was important he saw that this time I held the trumps. Now I saw it was true; he might have himself under control, but he was on edge.

"Martyn Carthy said you were coming because you had

something to give me," he said. "I can't imagine what it can be."

His profession of ignorance irritated me, it was so pointless. "Why pretend you don't know?" I said.

He hadn't suggested we sit down, and for a moment we looked into each other's eyes. His were watchful, almost expressionless.

"The envelopes."

"Yes."

"What makes you think they're important to me?"

"The lengths you've gone to to get them back. When you saw them in your wife's deed-box you nearly passed out. And you phoned Caroline to ask her to find them. A minister with a crisis on his hands whose wife has just been murdered, and you say they weren't important?"

"Caroline?" He might never have heard of her, but I knew he was sounding me out, trying to discover how much I knew.

"Yes," I said.

"You say she told you I'd asked you to get them back?"

"Not in so many words."

He walked over to the fireplace and leaned one elbow on the mantelpiece. It was a theatrical pose, but it seemed natural enough the way he did it. He was playing for time, and the realization gave me something else to worry about.

"Where's Roberts?" I demanded.

"Roberts?" He seemed genuinely surprised.

"The plain-clothes man who's been following me for the last week," I told him.

Sapsed was staring at me as if he didn't know whether to believe I was serious or not. Perhaps he was afraid I was. "Are you mad?" he asked.

"No. Though lately I've begun to wonder," I admitted. "What is he? Special Branch?"

Sapsed ignored the question; I hadn't expected him to answer it. "It was your own fault," he said flatly.

"Look," I told him, "since I've had those envelopes my house has been searched twice, my chairs have been ripped open, a friend who went to see what was happening was knocked out, my room at the Lamb has been gone over and I've been arrested on a trumped-up charge. My father-in-law's house has been searched while he was visiting his wife in hospital; they think she has cancer. I hope that makes you feel better."

"I'm sorry," Sapsed said. "Where are they now?"

I took them from my pocket and handed them to him. He took them and counted them while I watched him.

"There are only eleven here," he said.

"I've kept the others—just in case."

"In case of what?"

"Just in case."

"You could find yourself in serious trouble."

"I'm used to it. Anyway, for what? According to you, you haven't been trying to get your hands on them and, in any case, they aren't yours, they belong to Mrs. Sapsed's estate. Strictly speaking, I shouldn't have given you those."

He was turning them over in his hands, looking at them almost as if they no longer interested him. Perhaps they didn't, now he had recovered them. "I suppose you've thought up some lurid reason for my wanting them back?" he said.

"I know your wife was blackmailing you."

"She found out about Caroline. You didn't know Rosemary; she had to destroy people."

"Like her first husband," I said.

He gave me a quick, angry look. "You have done your homework, haven't you?" he commented contemptuously.

"It was a question of survival."

"Survival?"

"Mine."

He seemed to consider that, then decided to let it pass. "People expect politicians to live by a different set of rules. To observe standards they're not prepared to observe themselves. It's hypocritical."

"It wasn't Caroline," I said. "If that had come out you could have lived with it; plenty of other MP's have. It might have cost you a few votes, but it's a long time to the next election."

Unexpectedly, although I had kept three of the envelopes and they represented as great a potential danger to him as the whole fourteen, it seemed to me he had relaxed. Perhaps my handing over the others without wanting anything in return had reassured him.

"We may as well sit down," he observed, taking one of the easy-chairs.

I took one facing him. "It was Czechoslovakia, wasn't it?" I asked. "A girl?"

He hesitated. Perhaps he was wondering how much I knew and how much more it was safe to tell me.

"Yes." He spoke so quietly I hardly heard him. "It was in Dubček's time. There was a wonderful atmosphere in Prague then; it was like the end of winter and everybody realizing spring has come. I'd gone to do some research at the university. She worked there. It was a long time before I learnt she worked for the KGB, too."

"And your wife found out."

"Yes."

He hadn't gone to the police, because he knew that, however discreetly the matter was handled, something would inevitably leak out and his career would be finished. So he had gone on paying up and borrowing more and more heavily from the bank to do so.

"You knew it was her when you saw the envelopes in her box?" I asked.

He nodded. "I had no idea until then. I suppose she enjoyed the feeling of power it gave her. Perhaps she couldn't really help it; there was something tormented about her at times and she had to hurt people. Lately it had been getting worse."

I wondered if, even now, he realized the full extent of her perfidy; she had set out quite deliberately to wreck his career and make him a poor man, not openly but secretly, treacherously. He had called her tormented; in the old days they would have said she was possessed of the devil.

"Who else knows about the girl in Prague?" I asked him.

There was a noticeable pause before he answered, "The Prime Minister—and one or two of the security people, I suppose."

"When did you tell them?"

"When I got to the House on Friday—after I'd seen you and that other chap here. It's been out of my hands since then. I didn't know what they were doing."

I might know next to nothing about the machinery of government and how it worked, but I could guess at the consternation his disclosure must have caused. It could hardly have come at a worse time. Whatever happened, the blackmail and his affair in Prague had to be kept quiet; it must never be known that Britain's Defence Minister was vulnerable to that kind of pressure. The envelopes must be recovered. For the first time I really understood the danger I had been in, and my blood ran cold. For the simplest, most effective way of hushing up the whole business would have been to eliminate me. Only, then they might never have known where the envelopes were hidden.

I guessed it had been the Prime Minister or someone close to him, perhaps the head of DI6, who had told the Chairman to warn me off. They hadn't wanted any more drastic action taken—in case, from a sense of grievance, I had talked about what I knew. They couldn't know how little it was then and that their warning and Roberts' actions had had the opposite effect to that which they had intended.

"You didn't think it was the KGB blackmailing you?" I asked.

"I didn't know who it was at first. But they wouldn't have wanted money."

He had a point there. Also, when he went to Prague he was an obscure economics lecturer who had given up his job; they wouldn't have known what he would become.

"How did you get involved in all this?" he demanded.

I told him. "And because it looked as if you had killed your wife and it was going to be hushed up," I ended.

"You thought that?"

"Why not? You had two good motives: she had been blackmailing you, and you needed the money you expected her to leave you."

"I told you, I didn't know it was her until I saw the envelopes in her box."

"I couldn't be sure of that."

"You still think I killed her?" He stood up and turned, looking down at me. From where I was sitting he looked big and powerful.

The first scud of rain spattered the windows and I realized how dark it had become.

"No," I answered. "I know you didn't."

Outside, lightning forked, seeming so close it must strike the house. The thunder came almost simultaneously, crashing with a violence that almost deafened me.

"You know who did?" Sapsed asked.

"Yes."

I was convinced then that he had guessed himself but

wasn't sure; yet he didn't ask me. Instead he went off at a tangent.

"It's all over between Caroline and me. I haven't seen her since—"

"Have you told her so?"

"She knows."

I wondered, and wished I had his confidence. Rain slashed the windows. It was torrential now, but I had a sudden urge to get away. I had done what I came to do, but the evening was not over yet and there remained one thing more. I looked at Sapsed; what horrors haunted him?

"I'm going," I told him. Then, almost without intending to, I added, "Will you come with me?"

I thought he was going to refuse, but after a second's hesitation he said simply, "Very well."

He went for his coat. When he returned he was carrying an umbrella, too. Sheltering under it as best we could, we ran to the Triumph. His car might have better fitted his ministerial dignity, but presumably it was locked in the garage. As I opened the driver's door, lightning flared again and thunder slammed my ears. I could hear the rain drumming on the hood as I leaned across to open the other door for Sapsed.

"God!" he exclaimed.

I switched on the headlights, then the ignition.

We met no other car in the lane, and the streets of the Old Town were deserted; not even mad dogs and Englishmen went out in weather like this if they could avoid it. The rain fell in a nearly impenetrable sheet, pounding on the Triumph's hood and bouncing off the road. The gutters had become fast-flowing streams, and already in places the road was under water.

There were lights on in the flats. I stopped as close to the doors as I could, but still we had to run twenty yards through the downpour, and by the time we reached the lobby my jacket and trousers were soaked. We stood there, panting, trying to brush the rain off our clothes. Neither of us had spoken since that muttered exclamation of Sapsed's.

A notice by the lift-door said, "Out of Order." I swore under my breath and turned towards the stairs, Sapsed following me.

Our shoes made wet prints on the treads. I was conscious of a tension inside me which had nothing to do with running through the rain, and on the landing we stood and looked at each other. Sapsed's eyes were accusing.

"Why didn't you tell me?" he demanded.

"You knew," I told him. "That's really why you haven't seen her since it happened, isn't it? You couldn't face her."

He didn't answer, and I rang the bell. There was no response and I tried again, keeping my finger pressed on the button until my flesh went dead, but if there was anybody at home they weren't going to open the door.

"Well?" Sapsed asked.

There was a light on inside the flat. I had seen it from the car and I could see it now, a thin strip of light at the bottom of the door.

"We've got to get in," I said.

Sapsed looked at me and I expected him to tell me not to be a fool, but perhaps something he saw in my face stopped him. He put a hand in his pocket and produced a bunch of keys, selected one and inserted it in the lock. When he pushed the door, it opened.

Caroline was in the bath. She hadn't any sleeping-pills, so she had used a carving knife. It was almost new; she must have bought it to replace the one with which she had stabbed Rosemary Sapsed, and it probably seemed appropriate to her she should use it on herself. There wasn't much blood; neat to the last, she had stripped to her bra and briefs and turned the cold water on to wash it away. Perversely, that made it seem worse somehow.

I wanted to be sick. I heard Sapsed mutter, "Oh, God!" and turned away. He leaned over her, feeling for a pulse, but I think we both knew it was no good; she must have been dead some time.

I went back to the living-room. There was a half-empty whisky bottle on the table and an empty glass beside it. I wondered how much whisky there had been in the bottle before and tried not to think of her sitting there, drinking purposefully, waiting for it to take effect before climbing into the bath, knife in her hand.

There was something else on the table: an envelope. To my surprise, I saw it was addressed to me, and picked it up. The note it contained was brief and characteristically to the point: she had killed Rosemary Sapsed. It was clear from what I had said this afternoon I knew that and she couldn't face the humiliation of a trial and its inevitable sequel. No expression of remorse, nor of regret for herself. No mention of Sapsed.

He came out of the bathroom and I stuffed the note and the envelope in my pocket.

"She did it to protect me," he said. It showed how little he understood her, but if it made him feel better I didn't mind. "How did you know it was her?"

He couldn't have killed his wife; even in the late evening, when there was less traffic, it would have taken him at least forty minutes to drive from his house to Westminster, park his car and walk to the Chamber, and he had been seen there at ten thirty. As for Hillyer, I had believed him when he said Rosemary Sapsed hadn't told him about her new will; she wouldn't have trusted him to keep it to himself. Perhaps, even, not to kill her for her money. I suspected she had never intended him to inherit it; she hadn't expected to die. The will was a joke with herself, a way of hurting her husband still more if anything should happen to her.

Carthy had seemed more likely; he was emotional and he had suffered at her hands that night. But if he had taken a knife with him—and why should he?—surely he would have used it then, not gone out to the wood and waited there on the off-chance she would come that way? By the time she did, his bitter anger would have degenerated into self-pity.

I had wondered about the French girl, but the police must have satisfied themselves she was innocent.

It was a long time before I considered Caroline as a possible culprit, but she had had good reason to hate the dead woman. She had seen what Rosemary Sapsed was doing to her husband and perhaps she had hoped that with her out of the way he would marry her. She might even have counted on his inheriting his wife's money. Above all, she possessed the resolution and the ruthlessness to go through with it.

She and Sapsed had been careful, so discreet nobody seemed to know about their affair; yet, according to her, they had been together here when Rosemary was killed. Why should he have taken the risk of being seen entering or leaving her flat just at that time? It was only this afternoon in the train returning from London I had seen that in seeming to provide an alibi for him she had provided one for herself and that he couldn't have been with her and still been in the House of Commons at ten thirty. Lately she must have been tortured seeing the trouble she had brought on him. Women like her didn't love easily or often, and when they did it could spell danger, for them and for other people.

I remembered her saying that some people believed all murderers were mad and asking if I thought so. And I had told her that to me murder seemed the ultimate selfishness.

"Have you been here often?" I asked Sapsed.

"No, this is the first time. We usually met in London; I have a flat there."

"You have a key."

"She wanted me to have it." He hesitated and added awkwardly, "I think it made her feel—"

"More sure of you?"

"That we belonged together. Something like that." He looked haggard and several years older.

"You'd better go," I told him. "I'll call the police."

"I can't."

"Why not? What good will your staying do? Have you got a death-wish or something?" I was angry; I was doing my best to protect him and he wanted to be noble.

I could see the effort he made to pull himself together. "Very well," he agreed, "I suppose you're right. Thank you."

From the window I watched him emerge through the swing-doors and walk away down the hill. The rain had slackened, but he had his umbrella up; nobody would recognize him. I let the curtain fall back into place and went to ring the police.

The next morning I spent restoring as much order as I could at home. The worst damage couldn't be hidden, other would require skills I didn't possess to put it to rights, but by the time I had finished, the rooms looked better than I had been afraid they would. It was gone half-past twelve; I went next door for Nigel and together we walked up the road to the pub.

During the afternoon, Laura rang to say she was at King's Cross and would be on the train which arrived at Cressford at three fifty if I still meant it about meeting her.

The NATO crisis was resolved at the Ministers' meeting. Officially Rosemary Sapsed's murder was never solved. I destroyed the letter Caroline had left me in case it fell into the wrong hands and her affair with Sapsed became public knowledge. Her suicide was written off as tragic and unexplained.

I heard no more about the charges against me except that they had been dropped.

Three weeks later Sapsed resigned "for personal reasons." The papers published the letters between him and the Prime Minister, who had accepted his resignation with "very great regret, both personally and for the country." I wondered how much pressure had been put on Sapsed to resign and remembered something he had said the afternoon Bates and I called to see him: that the trouble with being a politician was that even sincerity became a sort of hypocrisy.

ABOUT THE AUTHOR

IAN STUART is a successful writer living in England. He is the author of nine previous mystery novels. *The Garb of Truth* is his first novel for the Crime Club.